In His Eyes

ELLA JUSTICE

Editing, typesetting and ebook production by
Ten Thousand | Editing + Book Design
www.tenthousand.co.uk

Cover design by Rena Violet
www.coversbyviolet.com

*To those who want to run from their darkness,
yet fight to stay for those they love in the light.*

CHAPTER ONE

Fight or flight. Fight is perceived as stronger; often seen as the brave approach. But flight can be smart too. Powerful even. For me? My flight response had always been on, and there was nothing powerful about it. It felt like I'd spent my whole life running. And here's what I'd learned about fight or flight so far—it wasn't a choice you made; it was a choice that got made for you.

"Ari, are you hungry?" Mom's voice pulled me out of my thoughts. Barely glancing over at her in the passenger seat, I gripped the steering wheel and slightly shook my head.

We were still more than a few long hours from Avila Beach, California. Our destination. Our refuge. Stopping felt out of the question, even though Mom had tried to convince me to at least pull over. I couldn't. Fear had warped my mind, and I was wide awake. The sooner we got there, the safer we'd be. At least, that was our hope.

"You sure you're okay to keep driving, sweetheart?" My mom placed a gentle hand on my arm.

She'd finally gotten some sleep and looked less exhausted, but I could still see the fear in my eyes reflected in hers.

"Yeah, Mom, I'm fine. We're gonna have to stop for gas in a little bit, and I'll get some more energy drinks. I'll be good."

"You need to get some rest, Arielle. This isn't healthy. You haven't slept since—"

"I'll sleep when we're safe. Have you called Sarah yet?"

She ran a nervous hand through her matted hair as she looked away from me, out the window, turning our only burner phone over and over in her hands—we'd had to leave our personal cell phones behind. I knew she hadn't called her yet.

Now it was my turn to put a comforting hand on her arm and give her an encouraging smile. "She'll be so excited to see us again. I'm sure of it."

"I don't know, I just feel like we abandoned them when they needed us most—when they were relying on us so heavily for support. And we just never came back."

"Sarah understood why we couldn't. Once we moved to Kansas, we couldn't afford the trips anymore. In a lot of ways."

My hands grasped the steering wheel even more tightly. Sarah wasn't the one I was nervous about seeing. But I tried to dismiss the thought as soon as it popped into my mind. *Just keep driving.*

"She's going to be so surprised by how much you've grown." She ran a hand lovingly over my hair as she spoke.

I gave her a timid yet warm smile. The sun was starting to set, and the sky was full of soft oranges and pinks. It caught my mom's strawberry-blonde hair, making it look as if it were on fire. Her hair had much more red in it than mine, but that just made her blue eyes even more striking and her small, upturned nose even more fitting. She was small, but she was strong. Brave. She was all I had.

"Mom?"

"Hm?"

"I'm still scared."

I could see tears glistening in her eyes and felt my own tears swell to the surface. I pushed the vivid images back down into the oblivion where they belonged. We hadn't really discussed what we were running from, and we weren't naive enough to believe that our past would stay safely behind us. But we were naive enough to believe we had time.

Long after the sun had gone down, I finally gave in and pulled over on the side of the highway so I could sleep. I wouldn't admit it, but I was exhausted. The fear that had been keeping me awake had also wiped me out. I quickly fell asleep in the uncomfortable driver's seat, leaving my mom with the passenger seat.

Our small five-seater had seats that reclined all the way back, and while we had no pillows or blankets, I still refused to stay at a hotel. Too much information. Too easy to track. We paid for everything in cash, but a hotel required a name and ID, and that was too much of a risk. Mom didn't even try to fight me on it. I got my stubbornness from her, but we could both recognize a wasted argument when we saw it. Fear creates confusion, but it can also create clarity.

I woke up to the sound of a muffled voice. I blinked until my eyes finally opened then took in my surroundings. Cramped car. Energy-drink cans. Mom, talking on the burner phone. Her voice became clear as my foggy mind finally woke up.

"I know it's last minute—you sure it's alright? … I know, she's excited to see you too. You won't believe how much she's grown. … Of course, he's practically a man. We're about an hour away, but we're gonna make a quick stop before we get to your place."

There was a pause, and I stretched my arms above my head as Mom glanced my way. Her tight smile told me all I needed to know.

"I know it's a strange number—yeah. … Yeah don't worry we're okay. … Is it okay if I fill you in when we get there? …

Thank you so much. Really. You have no idea how much we appreciate this. See you in an hour or so? … Okay, bye. Love you too."

She hung up the phone and rolled down her window. Crisp, cool air just barely warmed by the sun drifted into the car. The sun was bright in the sky, so it was probably ten in the morning at least. We would make it to Sarah's by lunchtime.

"What did she say?" I asked as I reached for the knob that controlled my seat, returning it to a sitting position. Our one duffle bag was sitting wide open in her lap, and she had clothes strewn across the dashboard. "And how long have you been up?"

"She's excited to see us, though I think she's a bit concerned."

Tactfully, she'd ignored my last question. By the dark bags under her eyes, I already knew the answer. And even though I knew I shouldn't, I felt guilty about sleeping so long.

"About the lack of notice, or that we're coming?"

"Both probably. A cross-country road trip isn't really our usual thing, sweetheart."

She took a deep breath then pulled out our lone shampoo bottle. "I couldn't sleep, so I got to thinking and figured we could probably use a quick wash-up before we head over there. Make a good impression."

"And so we don't kill them with our stench."

She gave me a tentative laugh and pulled out the deodorant.

"Never fear, my darling daughter, we will fight the hippie-road-trip smells together."

We both laughed a little at that. I appreciated her staying light and upbeat. It was the best we could do, and all we had to cling to was whatever optimism and hope we could find to try and drown out the darkness and fear. It was a constant, ever-present battle of the mind. It always had been for us.

I turned the key in the ignition and checked my face in the rearview mirror as the engine roared to life, reaching a hand tentatively to my sad excuse for hair.

"It might take more than some deodorant to fix all this."

"Once we get about twenty minutes out, there's some indoor surf showers we can use. If memory serves me right, they're actually pretty nice. A little busy, but I think we can both agree it's worth it."

I smiled at her continued effort to be positive, but I could also hear the tremor in her voice and see the shaking of her hands.

The mental battle continued.

"Okay, let's get going. And I get to pick the station today—I'm not sure how much more Nirvana I can handle."

"They are timeless!"

She gaped at me, but I saw real joy in her eyes. Nothing made my mom happier than arguing about music. It was her ultimate happy place.

"I need some chill-out vibes, not 'mommy didn't hug me when I was a child.'" As I pulled back onto the freeway, I turned the radio to the classical music station. Beethoven soothed me the way rock soothed my mother, and I desperately needed some soothing.

CHAPTER TWO

It seemed to take forever to get to the surf showers, but when we finally pulled in, I was surprised at how many people there were. A flash of brown hair and a muscular back stood out from the crowd, and fear shot through me. I clutched the wheel tightly. Mom saw my fear and quickly reached for my hand, dragging it from my fierce hold on the wheel and pulling me round to face her.

"Hey, breathe, sweetheart," she said as she ran a soothing hand over my hair. "Breathe. It's not him. It's some random surfer guy. It's not him."

Taking a deep breath, I looked down in embarrassment. My body had reacted before my brain. Again. That's what had gotten us here in the first place. I offered Mom a small smile as I felt warmth creep over my face.

"I'm supposed to be the logical one. Look at you, calming me down," I said as I slowly released another shaky breath.

A soft smile graced her lips, but concern laced her eyes. And fear. The same fear was still there, as if she was doing the same thing I was. Fighting to breathe. Fighting to appear calm. Another split second, and the fear was hidden. We'd had years of practice smothering emotions.

"Come on. Let's get my beautiful daughter looking, and smelling, gorgeous again."

After quickly climbing out of the car, we walked arm in arm to the shower stalls. The number of people around us was crushing. I held close to my mother, my wary eyes darting around for any sign of danger. I could feel the tension in my mother's grasp as she pulled me even closer, steadfastly avoiding eye contact with anyone.

After what felt like an eternity, we finally reached the showers. A breath I hadn't realized I'd been holding came rushing out, and my mother let out her own sigh of relief. She pointed to two stalls in the corner, away from the only other two people in this section of the showers, then gave my hand a tight squeeze and handed me our little bottle of shampoo. I silently thanked the universe for inspiring people to build giant communal beach showers, no matter how useless and touristy they'd felt to me before.

Inside the stall, warm water rushed over me, and I let myself get lost in the stream of heat as it hit my chilled skin—closing my eyes and fading into the clean, peaceful feeling that washed over me. But when I ran my hands up over my face and through my hair, that peace was slightly broken by the reminder of why I needed a shower in the first place.

I grabbed the shampoo bottle and started the laborious task of washing my filthy hair, but as I scrubbed the soap into my scalp, I started to feel anxious. Worried. My chest tightened. My breathing got a little faster. After the first wash, I still felt grimy.

It wouldn't come off—that grimy feeling. It was stuck. And all the memories of that night came flooding back to me as I frantically scrubbed the nonexistent scum away.

It. Would. Not. Come. Off.

The heat was suddenly suffocating. I tried to slow my breathing. My hand shot out, trying desperately to steady my body against the wall. Images, like a movie, started flashing through my head—one, then another and another and another, until I was overwhelmed, like my brain had been stretched to its limit trying to see and feel and ignore everything at once.

I gasped for air. The shampoo bottle dropped to the floor, the solid thud echoing against the tile.

"Ari? You good, sweetheart?"

Mom's voice opened my lungs and brought me back to the present. I looked around and took in my surroundings. Tiled shower stall. Shampoo bottle lying on the floor. The steamy water. I wasn't there. What had set me off?

I took another gulp of air. *Breathe. Just breathe. Safe. Safe. I am safe.* Another gulp of air.

"Yeah, yeah, I'm fine. Switch?"

She was silent, and I could almost feel her trying to decide how to respond.

She quietly rolled the body wash under the door as I rolled the shampoo to her.

Everything was fine. My mom was okay. I was okay. We were almost to Avila Beach and then we would be truly safe. But the nagging fear that nothing was okay kept bombarding me.

I quickly ran the body wash over myself then let the water cascade over me one last time before I slammed the knob down, stopping the stream of water. It was no longer peaceful. It was suffocating. He ruined everything.

"Hey, Mom, I'm done."

"Okay, sweetie, you dry off and get dressed first."

I reached under the door separating the stalls, pulled the bag to my side, and rifled through until I found the towel and my clothes.

We each only had one change of clothes. I pulled out a pair of jean shorts and one of my old white shirts. It had long, flowing sleeves and was slightly cropped so it made my waist look smaller. I laughed a little in spite of myself, remembering a time when the most important thing to me had been looking skinny and having clear skin. Sadness pierced me—those simpler days seemed like heaven. I tugged the shorts on and pulled the shirt over my head, slipping on my flip-flops as I did so.

Looking down, I slowly put the towel back into the bag before sliding it back to Mom's stall. She'd had this bag packed for months. I'd never known where she'd hidden it, but I'd known it existed. I'd hoped we'd be able to use it someday. As much as I hated to admit it, we'd both been planning our escape in little ways for years.

"Trying to make us look ready for the beach?" I asked, jolted from my thoughts as I heard her water turn off.

"Well, missy, we are ready for the beach. The sun. Our friends. A little normal. All of it."

"Welcome to Avila Beach," I muttered, but I couldn't hold back the sarcasm in my voice. I wasn't sure I wanted to act like everything was normal. I wanted to show my anger and fear. Let myself drown in the angst and the bitterness of the world doing me wrong. But that wasn't me. I had to be Mom's happy little Arielle. For her, I couldn't let the shock of what happened change me. Or at least, I had to act like it hadn't.

Mom stepped out of her stall and called for me to follow her. There were some mirrors by the doors to the showers. She handed me a brush, and I got to work taming my tangled locks while staring at my reflection.

My long, wavy blonde hair was almost to my waist now, and had more brown than strawberry blonde, courtesy of my dad. My green eyes, also courtesy of my dad, were filled with fatigue, and I suddenly realized that I looked almost nothing like my mom. The only way you could tell we were related was the upturned nose. And the stubborn spirit. That was our strongest resemblance. I smiled at her through the mirror.

"Ari, you and me. You and me." She smiled and gave me a hug from the side as we studied our attempt at pulling ourselves together. This was our mantra—what we said to each other whenever we needed it.

"Always, always."

"Let's get on the road, shall we? Knowing Sarah, they were expecting us an hour ago."

As we made our way back to the car, I glanced out at the water. I knew that the surf was starting to get good, so everyone was going to hit the waves. Even the tourists could sense the urgency to be in the water—to be a part of the energy that surrounded it. With a sad smile, I thought of the summer days I'd been right there with them, fighting for the best waves and a position in the masses. It felt like another life.

We hopped back in the car, and I insisted on driving again. Sarah's house was close, and I didn't see the point in messing up my groove. My mom insisted that we play her nineties music—she didn't see the point in messing up *her* groove.

As we drove along the beautiful coast to our second home, for the first time in a long time, we rolled down the windows and let our hair fly.

Sarah's house was deep in a neighborhood full of little beach shacks, on a long winding road to the beach that split into two. One track headed to the parking lot for beachgoers and the other to Sarah's place. I'd always wondered how Sarah had managed to get such an amazing place, considering she was a schoolteacher and didn't make much money. Or really care for material things in the slightest. Last time I'd asked, she'd simply winked and told me I wasn't quite old enough to know that story.

As we took the road to her place, I felt a wild mix of emotions. Every summer of my childhood had been spent here. Every happy memory I had was made here. I'd been only twelve when we left for the last time, and so much had happened since. So much I hadn't yet faced. But that was the funny thing about life: whether or not you were ready, some things had to be faced.

As we pulled up the drive, a very familiar woman paced back and forth on her white wrap-around porch, which was my favorite part of the faded two-story yellow beach shack.

Calling Sarah "eccentric" wouldn't do her justice. With her full head of wild brown curls always bouncing and her relentless positive attitude, she and my mother balanced each other out perfectly. The amount of energy that coursed through Sarah's thin, wiry body was a mystery, considering life hadn't been easy on her—the same way its rougher side had taken to Mom. Their friendship was something that had lasted a lot of long, hard years despite it all. Sometimes, I felt like it was the only thing that kept them going. I loved the safety of it.

"Here—park right here, sweetheart."

I parked where my mom pointed, and she grabbed my arm and gave me a smile.

"Jess! Oh my goodness gracious!" Sarah came walking quickly from the porch as soon as my mom stepped out of the car, hands fluttering excitedly around her face. Mom took a few steps towards her before they caught each other in a tight hug. Tentatively, I grabbed our bag and stepped out of the car as well, nervously tucking my hair behind my ears.

Sarah and my mom were laughing and talking to each other excitedly like they always did when they got together as I walked around the front of the car. Mom saw me and gestured for me to come over.

"And you remember my little Arielle."

The words had hardly left her mouth when Sarah let out a squeal and grabbed both of my hands in hers.

"Not so little anymore, Jess. No, this can't be my little Ari whose only dream was to be a surf goddess."

She looked into my eyes, and I felt the same comfort I'd felt around her when I was little. Sarah always had this warmth about her, this light in her blue eyes that comforted any lost soul.

"The same, Auntie Sarah. Although I think my dreams have changed a little bit."

"Oh, I hope not! I always thought you would make an incredible surf goddess," she exclaimed enthusiastically.

I gave her a genuine smile, and she turned towards the house and motioned for us to follow. We walked up the stairs then she opened the door, ushering us in. Mom entered first, looking lighter than she had in years—like a burden had been lifted simply by being here.

"Sarah, thank you so much for accommodating us on such short notice," Mom said, giving her an embarrassed smile that Sarah just waved away with her animated hands.

"Oh stop thanking me before I get a hostess complex. We were so excited when you called! I prepped your usual rooms, and your lunch is being made right now!"

As we walked past the living room towards the kitchen, I breathed in the sweet scent of Sarah's world-famous fish tacos. My stomach growled without my permission, and I looked sheepishly at the two women as they both let out a giggle.

"I'm guessing that's a yes to lunch then. Straight on to the kitchen!" Sarah exclaimed.

Now I giggled with them.

"Hey, Ma, I was thinking maybe we—"

The boy that turned around when we entered stopped his sentence short when he saw my mom and I standing there. Only he wasn't a boy anymore. Not at all. Not even close.

He was taller than the last time I'd seen him, with more muscles and no acne. His chestnut hair curled a little, just enough to add a boyish look to his otherwise very not boyish body. He had high cheekbones and these piercing blue eyes that had always given me butterflies. His skin was always tanned, and now it was smooth and perfect. Even just standing there with a spatula in his hand, he was so handsome it hurt.

We stood there, just staring at each other for what seemed like an eternity. Then I saw that twinkle in his blue eyes I remembered from when we were kids. A mischievous smile stretched across that beautiful face, and in a split second, he was over to me and lifting me off the ground in a big hug.

Nathaniel Rentz, my best friend from my childhood, was all grown up.

CHAPTER THREE

Surprised, I grabbed on for dear life and laughed as he spun us in a circle.

"Nate, come on, put me down."

But he spun me around one more time and I couldn't help but let out another laugh as he put me gently back on the ground. I stepped back quickly but couldn't hide my smile from him.

"Wow, Arielle Hansen. I—I—uh—"

He scratched the back of his head, looking me up and down. His eyes lit up, like he'd found something he liked. Um, was he checking me out? There's no way.

"You what?" I questioned, putting my hands on my hips as I waited.

He opened his mouth then glanced over at our mothers, who were looking at us like they were watching one of the romance movies they used to put on every night. I shook my head at them. Nate was just an old friend. Who I'd been in love with since I was six. Yep.

"I'm taller than you now," he said triumphantly.

"Finally. It only took you, what, seventeen years to catch up?"

"What? Not even close!" He looked at me in mock shock. "It only took me fifteen to catch up—the other two were me getting ahead."

"Yeah, okay. Just keep telling yourself that."

As I spoke, my mom hooked arms with Sarah, and they walked over to the stove that Nate had left unattended.

"Hey, Nate, why don't you grab some chips and take my Ari girl down to the beach for a little bit. Remind her what she's been missing out on while I have a talk with her mama," Sarah said, gesturing to the open sliding glass door. I could see the beach past the flowing white curtains.

My heart was gripped with irrational fear. I hadn't been apart from my mom since that night. I looked over at her, and she met my eyes with certainty, her lips pressed into a thin line. This was allowed. I could go outside. This was perfectly normal.

With Sarah to talk to and the beach in view, she felt safe. There was no clinging to fear, no constantly looking over her shoulder, no being afraid to speak unless spoken to. This home—Sarah and Nathan's home—this was our safe space. Our sacred ground. Mom felt it. But there was something more to her eyes as she smiled peacefully; a message she was trying to send me. And then it clicked that she wanted—no, needed—to fill Sarah in, without Nathan hearing everything. But I still hesitated.

She gave me a nod and gestured towards the door, telling me it was alright. I felt silly, but I was scared.

"You coming, Ari?" Nathan had already moved to the door, chips in hand, and was waiting for me to follow. He raised his eyebrows, confused by my hesitation.

"Yeah, sorry," I said under my breath as I tucked my hair behind my ears again and walked quickly out the door.

We walked in silence for a little bit; we'd taken our shoes off at the back door and were now kicking at the sand with our bare feet as we looked out at the horizon. Nostalgia came over me in waves as the salty scent hit my senses. These were beaches I'd loved, waves I'd played in. I could feel safe here too. The sky was a brilliant light blue, and it met with the dark blue of the ocean seamlessly. The water lapped over our feet as we walked away from the house. I'd missed this place. Seeing the water, feeling the salty breeze on my skin, it felt like being reunited with an old friend—exciting and terrifying and electric all at once.

I kept my gaze from Nathan as the thought raced through my mind.

"So, Ari, what's been going on?" he finally said, breaking the tense silence.

I gave him a noncommittal shrug. "Oh you know, I graduated high school at the end of May. Worked. Trying to figure out college. The normal stuff, I guess. What about you?" I couldn't look at him as the half-truths came out like they were second nature.

"Well I don't know if you've heard, but my surfing skills have improved greatly since you were last here and I can't keep the ladies off me. I've practically become a recluse simply for safety reasons, and it's only gotten worse since I got legal."

"Oh, gosh. Nathaniel Rentz, the king of humility. There's no way you could have improved that much since I left."

We laughed, and I felt safer than I had in months. This was us. Me and Nate. Walking along the beach like we used to, talking and joking like we always had. It was the same, yet everything was different.

"I guess you'll have to find out, surf goddess," he teased, smirking as he glanced over at me.

"It's Miss Surf Goddess to you," I retorted, trying not to notice how cute he looked when his eyes lit up as we joked. "Hey, I'm not the one who wanted to go to space and be the first person to eat cereal on Mars."

"Captain Crunch specifically. I was ten, and I stand by that as a pretty solid aspiration in life, *Miss* Surf Goddess!"

He pushed my shoulder, and my laugh caught in my throat at the electricity that shot through me. I tried to play it off, pushing my hair behind my ears and glancing up at him.

I found those blue eyes trained on me, a smile on his lips and a secret in his gaze, and my heart stuttered as I tried to find sense in the flurry of emotions that flooded my mind. The only thing it landed on, over and over, was a pull. Towards what I had no idea, but I was very sure who I felt pulled to. And my heart wanted him to keep smiling at me like that. Like the world would stop and it would all be okay if he'd still share that heart-stopping smile with just me.

"Hey, Rentz!" a shout rang out, interrupting my embarrassing train of thought.

Three tall guys in board shorts came walking towards us. Fear shot through me as I stumbled back, but Nate didn't seem concerned, so I didn't follow my initial instinct to run.

I took another glance at the approaching group—the one in the front looked vaguely familiar, but I couldn't place the other two at all. When they reached us, the first one looked me up and down, and suddenly broke into a grin. Then his arms swept me up into a big hug. My body tensed, immediately on edge at the unwanted physical contact. *Come on, Ari, just breathe.*

"Uh, hi. Um, Nathan…." I stuttered once I'd calmed down my immediate flight response, craning my neck to look at Nate with confusion and desperation. My face clearly screamed "help me."

Nate could only laugh, but it wasn't his normal, carefree laugh. It sounded strained, like he was just as on edge about this as I was.

"Johnny, put her down, man. She just got here and doesn't remember your ugly mug anyway."

The guy—Johnny apparently—set me down roughly and let out a noise of protest. I stumbled back, but Nate reached out to steady me then slid an arm around my waist. Every nerve in my body zeroed in on where he touched me, but this wasn't the time to get all mushy and sidetracked. I wasn't even sure what was happening here; whether or not I was in danger. I tried not to focus too much on how it felt having Nate's arm looped around me; instead, I stepped away, sizing up this Johnny guy. How did I know him?

I studied his lopsided grin and vaguely remembered a young, scrawny boy with dark hair and a bad attitude hanging around Nathan—his constant little shadow, always begging to play with us. That lopsided grin unlocked a distant memory.

"Wait, Johnny? The emo kid who would always try to surf with us?"

When Nathan nodded, Johnny let out another protest. "Oh, come on, you guys practically begged to hang out with me, and this is how I get remembered. Shameful, Arielle, just shameful."

"I'm sorry, Johnny. You really do look different. No braces, your hair is bleached, and I don't see any traces of your mom's eyeliner anymore. Who are you trying to be?" I tried to joke, sensing some weird feelings between this group and Nate. Johnny still hadn't introduced his friends, which was also weird.

Johnny's laugh suddenly turned deep and throaty, and he gave me that once-over look again—a slow scan up and down my body that made me want to hide. It wasn't friendly.

Nathan tensed beside me, and I shot him a questioning look as Johnny spoke again.

"Whoever you want me to be, baby girl." His eyes glinted, but not with a twinkle, like Nathan's did. This was dangerous, like he would take me when he wanted and throw me away when he was done. It made my skin crawl.

Nathan took an angry step forward, but I quickly put a hand to his chest, keeping my eyes on the suddenly very creepy Johnny.

"I just want you to be yourself. Whoever that is. See you later, Johnny." Without thinking, I grabbed Nathan's hand like when we were kids and dragged him past Johnny and his laughing friends. Nathan gripped my hand, and I knew that I was the only thing keeping him from turning around and punching the smug smile off Johnny's face.

We'd walked further down the beach towards the pier, away from Sarah's. I suddenly became very aware that I was still holding Nathan's warm hand in mine. I remembered how firm his chest had felt when I'd put my hand on it to stop him earlier; how the muscles in his arms had jumped into high definition when his hands tightened into fists.

Jeez, Ari, pull yourself together.

I felt heat rush across my face and almost jerked my hand from his grasp. He barely noticed. He was muttering under his breath and looking angrily at the ground as his hand dropped back to his side. Suddenly, he stopped walking. I turned to face him, but he wouldn't meet my eyes.

"I'm sorry, Ari. I know we were friends with Johnny when we were little, and I didn't mean to freak out on your first day here."

He turned to look out at the horizon, still avoiding my gaze. His words and the gruffness in his voice told me two very different things, so I shuffled my feet in the sand, not sure what to say.

We stood like that for a while, not speaking. Then I took a deep breath, only comfortable in speaking first because this was Nathaniel Rentz—he always listened to me, even when I rambled or ranted.

Tentatively, I reached my hand out and placed it gently on his arm. His eyes shot up to mine, and I did my best to hold them there. To ignore the flood of nervousness and excitement that seemed to occur whenever I touched this boy.

"Nate, why did he upset you so much?" I asked gently.

He looked away from me again, shaking his head. It felt like a rejection, so I let my hand fall.

"Please, I just want to understand. You're not a fighter. You don't get angry easily. When we were kids, I was always coming to your defense, and *you* had to pull *me* away from fighting with Johnny."

He let out a light laugh at that, looking up and giving me a knowing smile. And once again, I couldn't breathe. That smile. It was kind and mischievous and caring and teasing all at once. Jeez. I hadn't even been here an hour, and I was already starting to remember why I'd missed this place so much.

ARI. Get it together.

"I guess you were always the tougher one out of the two of us. I don't know—I just feel like I need to protect you. So you don't—"

He looked away from me again, and I could see his arm muscles tense up once more as he clenched his fists. I tucked my hair behind both ears and crossed my arms in a feeble attempt to protect my heart. Nathan had always been straightforward with me, honest even when I wished he wouldn't and complimentary right when he needed to be. It was an endearing yet annoying gift of his—one of many that had me feeling something too intense to be true.

"So I don't what?" I whispered, terrified to know and terrified to not.

"Ari." Another head shake.

He'd always been so sweet when it came to certain things. Like his honesty, it was perfect and infuriating all at once, especially when those all-seeing ocean eyes of his met mine with just enough kindness that made my heart flutter.

I dropped my hands in exasperation. "Nate, come on. You know you can tell me anything. We were best friends, you know."

He grabbed my hand, tight, like he always used to do when the waves got too big or his mom got mad at him, and I suddenly saw sunlight, soft and lazy, drifting through the glass windows as we ate donuts one morning. We could hear the waves crashing against the shore, and the seagulls were quiet. It was peaceful.

Then the crashing continued, but this time it came from upstairs. A suitcase, clothes flying out in every direction, tumbled down the stairs. Nate's father followed close behind, practically taking the steps two at a time as he ran. He shoved the clothes back in, yelled up the stairs, and walked out the door. He didn't even notice his son watching. Didn't even look back.

Witnessing such a dramatic scene had been so thrilling, I'd forgotten that eight-year-old Nathan was sitting next to me until I'd heard a sniffle. I'd looked at the tears in his big eyes, and my heart had broken swiftly in two. He'd grabbed my hand the same way he was doing now—hard and desperate, like the only thing anchoring him to this moment was me.

"Ari." Nathan's gentle voice jerked me back into the present. There were no tears in his eyes, but his expression was just as somber. "You're still my best friend."

I smiled. This was Nathan. *My* Nathan.

"You're still my best friend too. But you're avoiding the question. Why do you feel like you need to protect me?"

"So you don't leave again." He didn't hesitate; he didn't even pause to take a breath.

My heart pounded, my eyes prickled with tears, and I had to turn towards the ocean. Find my center, my peace. Find something to mellow the intensity.

It took me a moment to gather myself and my bravery.

Taking a deep breath, I slowly turned back towards him, and let my heart speak without letting me think. "Nate, I'm here."

It was all I could give him. As he smiled and turned contentedly towards the ocean, I didn't voice the second part of my thought. The part that rebounded in my head, calming me even as it filled me with fear.

But I can't promise that I'll stay.

CHAPTER FOUR

We walked the beach for another hour, catching up on life—mostly Nate's—and laughing about the stupid things we used to do as kids. It was always easy to get along with Nathan. We fell back into a steady rhythm as if nothing had changed. He really was still my best friend—I could feel that in every part of my soul.

When we got back to the beach house, Nirvana was blaring, and I could hear my mom and Sarah laughing and talking amiably. Nathan and I exchanged knowing grins, raising our eyebrows at each other as he slid open the glass door. We walked in to see both our mothers dancing and singing in the kitchen as they got the table set for lunch.

We stepped in front of the couches stuffed into the space along the edge of the room and moved towards the kitchen table. A vase of hydrangeas, Sarah's favorite flower, sat on the counter. Something about seeing those familiar flowers, right where they always sat, made me smile even harder.

Sarah was mid-chorus when she spotted Nate and I laughing and pointed at me. "Come on, little Ari, I know you know the words!"

I shook my head frantically. Little Ari. Too little. Too weak. She didn't mean it that way—I knew that. In my head, I knew that. She was my Auntie Sarah. But another voice took over.

You're so weak, little Ari.

What, you're just a little princess expecting everything to get done for you?

You think anyone could love you? You're not worth it, little girl.

Dizzy. Dizzy. Why did I keep doing this? I couldn't stop it. Black crowded the edges of my vision, and I reached out for a chair, for my mom, for anything. Then the whole world tilted.

I couldn't stop seeing it, over and over.

Bang, bang, bang.

Darkness.

Bang, bang, bang.

Run.

A single scream broke through the fog. Then the voice morphed, half in a memory and half pulling me out of it as it called my name.

"Arielle!"

I jerked my head forward as my eyes snapped open. Stars—I could still see stars. Then Mom and Sarah came into view, hovering in front of me, as the stars faded away. Mom's eyes were filled with worry; Sarah's eyebrows were pinched together.

Sarah's eyes moved quickly over mine as she tried to piece together what was happening. I felt a strong hand gently run over my hair, soothing and calm. I tilted my head back, and my gaze locked on a set of beautiful, concerned blue eyes. I suddenly realized that we were all on the floor, and my head was in Nathan's lap.

I sat up—too quickly.

"Whoa, whoa, baby girl. Take it easy, okay?" Sarah gently took my hand to help me up, then sat me down on the long bench that served as seating at their dinner table.

I put my hands on my head, fighting the fear that took my breath as Mom and Sarah sandwiched me on the bench. Mom rested a hand on my knee. Hesitantly, I lifted my eyes to meet hers.

"How many times, sweetheart?" she whispered. "How many times?"

"Three. Right now. In the showers, and then, when—when—" My hands started shaking again.

She grabbed my hand, effectively steadying it and calming my nerves all at once.

"I don't understand. I was fine. And then it just—I just—"

"It's okay, Ari baby. It's okay. You need to tell me when this happens, okay?" she pleaded, looking deep into my eyes.

I nodded, ashamed I hadn't told her before. But she didn't need to be worried about me when we had much bigger problems.

I heard a shuffle and glanced up to see Nathan standing by the doorway. His eyes were wide, and I knew he wouldn't see me as tough Ari anymore. In his eyes, I was glass. And I was getting closer and closer to the edge.

"I'm fine. Really, everything's okay. Everything's okay," I said, not sure who I was trying to convince. But I needed to convince somebody, or I'd never believe it.

I looked at all the concerned faces surrounding me. "Guys, come on. I think I'm just hungry. We've been living off gas-station food for the past few days, and I am in desperate need of some fish tacos. Right, Mom?"

I gave her a desperate look. I didn't know what she had or hadn't told Sarah, but I wasn't ready for Nathan to know. Not even close.

"Yes. Let's finish getting everything set up. Maybe we should eat outside in the fresh air," Mom said quickly, sensing my need to move on.

Sarah glanced at her, but Mom just shook her head in return. Eyebrows raised, Sarah gave my hand a squeeze then followed my mom back to the counter.

As I put my head back into my hands, resting my elbows on my thighs, I felt someone sit beside me. I didn't look up—I kept my eyes glued to the floor until a hand stretched in front of them.

"You want to go outside?"

I reached out hesitantly, but he grabbed my hand the way he always did. Like he'd never let me go.

We walked outside, hand in hand, and he showed me where they'd put the new outdoor table. It was pretty—white wood with a yellow umbrella. It matched the house. Nate gestured to the table, and I took a seat. He let go of my hand.

I wished he hadn't.

I knew he wanted to say something to me. There was so much I wanted to say to him. But I couldn't—and I knew I wouldn't.

"Are we going to talk about it?" he asked softly.

I avoided his eyes with all my might and gave a quick shake of my head.

"Okay, then can we at least act normal? This is too much."

I nodded enthusiastically. Normal was everything I wanted—what I craved.

I looked up to meet his eyes, and Nate leaned forward so our faces were inches apart. Scooting back, I inhaled sharply. What was that? Our lips could have touched if he'd leaned forward just a little bit more.

He kept moving forward. I was nervous he was going to kiss me and terrified he wouldn't.

Surprisingly, he stopped and smiled. Now I was just confused.

"What are you doing, Nathan?"

"Waiting for you to sass me. You said you were going to act normal."

I laughed and shoved him away from me. Good—now I could breathe.

"Oh, glad to see you guys are back to your usual roughhousing. As usual, I place my bet on my surf goddess," Sarah exclaimed as she stepped out of the house with a platter of heavenly fish tacos. My mom followed with a stack of plates and silverware.

As they set the food down, Nathan let out a sound of protest. "Come on, Mom—you've always chosen Ari over me."

His voice was playful, and I gave him a sweet smile and shrugged, which only made him groan again.

"Why, Nathaniel, you know I'm your number one cheerleader." Then it was Sarah's turn to smile as both women took a seat. "Except when you pick a fight with Ari. I can't cheer on a lost cause."

The laughter settled us, taking away the tension and giving us some semblance of normalcy, and as we started eating, everything started to feel relaxed again. The conversation was natural as we discussed the beach and what we'd missed in each other's lives—the parts socially acceptable to be spoken about when catching up with old friends. Normal. The small-talk kind of conversation where things are being said and things are being listened to, but the emotion rarely deviates from a contented, happy kind of comfort. The normalcy of it all calmed me.

"So, Ari, I hear you're quite the genius."

I almost choked on my fish taco, and Nathan gave me a hard pat on the back. I waved him off as he laughed at my attempt to regain composure.

"Well, Sarah, I think you've heard wrong." Still trying to catch my breath, I gave my mom a look, knowing full well she'd supplied that information. She was always so proud of anything I did. "Or someone greatly exaggerated my intelligence."

"What are you looking at me for, sweetheart? I didn't say anything about your extra AP classes, or your college courses, or your perfect ACT score, or your status as salutatorian at your old school. Not a word," she said sweetly, batting her eyelashes at me.

Sarah broke out into hysterical laughter.

"Guys, come on. I'm not a know-it-all."

"No one ever said you were," Nathan chimed in. "We were just thinking it."

This earned him another shove, but he just gave me his signature lopsided grin and kept munching on his fish taco. *Ugh. Boys.*

"Okay, funny guy, what have you been up to since I last saw you?"

"Oh, wait, I get to do an 'embarrass my son' moment!" Sarah clapped her hands and sprang from her chair as Nathan groaned and slumped down as far as his big frame would let him.

"You're in for it now," I leaned over and whispered.

He gave me a sardonic grin, but Sarah was already going off.

"So, Nathaniel has won several surfing competitions and also has left several broken hearts in his wake—"

"Ma!"

"Wait, honey, I'm not done yet." Sarah waved off all his forms of protest, and I raised my eyebrows at him. "He also has successfully graduated high school—didn't do as well as Ari, but he has other talents. Surprisingly, he loves photography! He is so insanely talented. Oh, and he hasn't stopped talking about how he hoped Arielle would come back since the moment she left."

Now it was my turn to be embarrassed. I looked down at my plate and felt my face flush again. He hadn't stopped talking about me? He hoped I would come back? My head was spinning. Why did he have this effect on me?

"Okay Mother, that's good. Really, I think that's more than enough."

His voice was strained, and I couldn't help but give Mom a smile. She started to open her mouth as well, and I knew what she was going to say. I had to stop it.

"Well, Nathan, you'll be surprised to find that—"

"I think it's time for us to clean up!" I practically yelled as I stood, my chair scraping loudly against the patio as I jolted out of my seat.

"Oh, come on, Ari. You haven't stopped talking about how much you missed Nathan either."

My mom's smile stretched ear to ear, and I knew she didn't feel bad in the slightest.

I felt Nathan's head whip around to face me. My face turned red again, and I quickly grabbed my plate. Sarah and my traitor mother stopped giggling long enough to see my movement and start to protest.

"Oh come on, sweetheart, we know you two are good friends. We're just trying to help you reconnect." Mom chuckled.

She looked so happy, laughing and smiling, that I had to smile back. Even though I didn't think I could ever make eye contact with Nate again.

"I know, Mom. We're old enough to do that on our own, you know."

"We are very much aware."

Mom had really gotten her spunk back. This place was magic.

Sarah burst into another round of giggles. I turned to walk into the house, shaking my head as I went. I pushed open the glass door, rounded the counter, and set my things in the sink. Then I turned on the water, grabbed the pans from the stove, and started washing them out. As I was scrubbing the first pan, a stack of plates landed beside me.

"You don't have to do that, Ari," Nathan said softly.

It bothered me, the care in his voice. He still saw me as glass.

"I know." I kept my back turned and continued to scrub everything away. "I like to help. It makes me feel useful, like I'm earning my keep."

He grabbed a dishtowel and started drying off the first pan I'd washed.

"You don't need to feel like you have to 'earn your keep.'" He put the dry pan away; I kept scrubbing. "Mom always says that you and Aunt Jess are welcome anytime."

"I know." Apparently that was the only coherent thought I had in my head. Great.

As I continued to try and ignore him, a sudden thought came to my head. I stopped scrubbing and turned to face Nathan, who'd paused because of my sudden movement. "Is it weird that we call each other's moms 'aunt' but we aren't related?"

Nathan laughed and started on the next pan.

"Nate, I'm serious. What if people think I'm your cousin? I love Sarah, but—"

"But what? Why are you concerned if people think you're my cousin?" He turned around to face me.

My throat went dry, and I couldn't meet his twinkling eyes. Why did his eyes always twinkle when I was uncomfortable?

"Um, well—"

"Ari."

At his soft voice, I looked up and found him closer than I thought. My breath caught in my throat. We were standing a mere few inches away from each other, and I could see his mind turning.

"Why are you trying to figure out what's in my head?" I whispered.

"Maybe I want to know."

He was staring too deep. Being too understanding, too caring, too much.

"I don't think you do." I couldn't hold his gaze anymore.

As soon as my eyes left his, he reached out and grabbed my hand. He really needed to stop doing that. Nathan had always held my hand when we were kids, but we weren't kids anymore. Maybe he was just a touchy guy? I shouldn't read into it. I really shouldn't.

Butterflies. So. Many. Butterflies.

"You always used to tell me everything," he whispered as his grip on my hand tightened.

I finally looked back up into the deep blue and found myself there. The way I was years ago, before all the mess. Before I grew up.

"When I'm with you, I feel like a little kid again," I whispered back. "Like I don't have to grow up just yet."

His gaze drifted to my lips. We were getting too close. Too intense. Too soon. But I wanted to fall for him. Completely. But how could I?

Then he grinned. "The little kid who used to beat me up or the girl who kissed me before she left and never said goodbye?"

I stepped away from him and pulled my hand from his grasp. Yeah, no. It was too soon.

"Yeah, um, I don't think we need to talk about that." I turned back to the dishes and began scrubbing again.

The door burst open, followed by a singing pair of moms who only saw me scrubbing away and Nathan standing there, looking lost.

CHAPTER FIVE

That night, after we'd cleaned up dinner, we sat around a bonfire on the beach. A few of Sarah and Nathan's friends joined us, which of course meant there were like thirty people. Apparently, it was a Sunday night tradition, and of course we didn't want them to change their plans for us.

Apparently, it was Sunday.

I could feel Nathan looking at me, trying to figure me out all over again. I had let him get too close. He was my best friend, but I'd only been here a day and we'd already had more than one deep talk. I'd hit my max.

Nathan sat across from me, talking to a couple of his surfing friends. Mom and Sarah were chatting with Sarah's friends, and I turned and watched the waves, the flames at my back.

I'd never minded being alone. All through high school, I stuck to myself mostly. I had one or two friends, but they weren't the kind of people I could talk to about real stuff. It was far more surface level. We talked about parties, grades, college plans, things anyone could know simply by checking your social media or asking a random classmate what they knew about you. Not that I had any social media or went to any parties or had any plans to go to college, but you get the idea.

It was so much safer to keep people at a distance. There was something peaceful about being left to your own thoughts. There was no pretending there, no faking it when you were totally alone. But then again, there was this deep longing I kept pushing away. For a long time, I didn't know what I was longing for. It hit me when I'd watched Sarah and Mom communicate without words before dinner. All I wanted was to be truly understood—I was tired of pretending.

"Ari!"

I turned around quickly, jarred out of my thoughts—Nathan was waving me over.

Taking a big breath, I walked around the fire. I was still in my shorts and white shirt, while Nathan was wearing the same shorts but had apparently lost his shirt. Huh. I was doing my best not to get distracted.

"Hey," I said hesitantly as I reached where he was standing. He was talking with two guys about our age, who both looked nice enough. They had also apparently lost their shirts. Did I also mention that boys had never really talked to me and those two friends in high school had been girls?

They could have been male models and my eyes would still have been stuck on Nate though.

Forcing myself to look away from my very muscular, very shirtless best friend, I tried to shake away the heat that was quickly rising to my cheeks.

"Ari, these are my buddies Kyle and Luke."

They each waved as their names were said. Kyle had shaggy, blonde hair and a goofy smile, while Luke had a shaved head and seemed too serious to be friends with the others.

"Kyle and Luke, this is Arielle."

"How ya doing, Arielle?" Kyle eagerly stuck out a hand.

I gently placed mine in his, and he shook it vigorously.

"I'm good, but you can just call me Ari. Everyone does," I said softly, giving them a small smile.

Luke stuck out his hand next and gave mine one firm shake.

"Nice to meet you, Ari. Good to know you actually exist." Luke pulled back his hand as he spoke and resumed his original position—arms crossed, feet wide. He reminded me of a security guard.

"What do you mean I 'actually exist'?" I looked at Nate, but he was too busy giving Luke the death stare.

Then Kyle jumped in. "He means Nate has been talking about this mystery girl ever since we met him back in freshman year, but we never met her and she was always conveniently without a phone, with no social media and across the country."

Nate gave Kyle a shove. He went on unfazed. "But here you are! Bam! To be perfectly honest, we thought he totally made you up."

I giggled—not at this new development but at Nathan's obvious discomfort.

"Why does everyone feel the need to say that today?" Nate mumbled under his breath.

I smiled sassily at an obviously disgruntled Nathan and turned to his friends. "I'm real, don't worry. Nate may be crazy, but he's not completely lost it yet."

Kyle gave me a disbelieving look, and I burst into laughter. Nathan grabbed my arm and pulled me towards the shore.

"Okay, you guys can't be friends!" he exclaimed as Kyle and I continued to laugh, and Luke watched on with a slight smile.

That felt like a big deal coming from him.

When we reached the water, I was breathless from laughing. Nathan stopped suddenly, and I almost fell over at the sudden change in momentum. He chuckled as I tried and failed to regain my balance. I felt all silly, like a schoolgirl in front of her crush, but Nathan wasn't my crush. I'd only been back a day, and I already knew he was so much more to me.

"If I didn't know better, I'd be worried you were drunk."

He tried to help me find my balance, but I tripped over my feet thanks to the loose sand and his sudden nearness. We fell into a giggling heap on the sand. The soft breeze blew my hair out of my face as Nathan struggled to untangle himself. We were both laughing hard as we rolled into a sitting position, facing the water.

We sat there for a minute, giggling like little kids and watching the waves swell and break against the sand. I saw a broken piece of shell at my feet and picked it up, running my fingers over the rough edges before tucking it in my pocket. I already had a few shell pieces in my pockets after our earlier walk on the beach. Apparently, some habits never died. Glancing over at Nate, my heart confirmed that sentiment.

After a minute of gazing at the ocean, Nathan looked at me. Then he quickly turned away again. He looked back two more times before I slapped his arm playfully.

"Ow! What was that for?" he exclaimed, his smile wide.

"Why do you keep looking at me?"

"Maybe I wasn't looking at you."

"Oh, no, you were just casually observing the sand behind me."

"Why, Ari, you know I can appreciate beauty when I see it. A good wave, a majestic sunrise, and of course—"

A sudden gust of wind blew a piece of hair in front of my face. Without even hesitating, Nathan reached up and tucked it behind my ear. But instead of quickly removing his hand and continuing his sentence, he cupped my cheek and leaned in closer, his eyes turning serious.

My breath caught in my throat, and I knew I should turn away. Nathan was someone I could always talk to. Someone who had always been there for me. Someone who made me vulnerable. It would be too easy to fall. And it would be too hard to pick up the pieces if it all fell apart. I needed to be strong.

But those eyes of his could see into my soul. My heart wanted something my head kept trying to fight. We'd been sitting there, clinging to our simple, uncomplicated and newly reformed friendship for what felt like an eternity, and now I had a choice. Lean in, give in to whatever this was—or lean back, keep away, and stay safe.

"Of course what?" I whispered, trying to break the spell.

We heard a loud shout behind us and jumped apart so quickly I barely had time to register that we were no longer touching. Nathan turned around, and I could have sworn I saw a hint of irritation on his face.

My choice was made for me.

"Hey, Ari, wanna dance?" Kyle shouted from the fire pit, where, sure enough, everyone was dancing around to one of my mom's favorite nineties songs whose name I'd intentionally blocked out of my mind.

He ran over to me like a goofy Labrador retriever and stuck out his hand. I grabbed it slowly, giving him a small smile.

"Sorry to steal your girl, Nate, but now that we know she exists, you can't keep her all to yourself."

He pulled me up roughly and dragged me to the fire pit, urging me to hurry up already.

But I couldn't. I'd left something really important on that beach, and I didn't quite know how to get it back yet.

After we'd done whatever Kyle declared was dancing, and sang and ate way too many s'mores, everyone turned in for the night. I hadn't had another chance to talk to Nathan. It seemed like everyone there wanted to ask about my plans now that I'd graduated high school, congratulate me on coming back or tell me a story about something I used to do on my yearly visits here. It was a lot—I was really, really awkward. It felt good to talk to someone other than my mom, Nate and Sarah, but I was drained. And overwhelmed.

Finally, I asked my mom if I could head in, and she decided to come with me. Sarah, endless energy powerhouse that she is, decided to put out the fire and send the stragglers home, only to suggest that we continue the party with just the four of us in the house, but I just wanted to sleep.

Mom, turning from where Sarah and Nathan were working to put the fire out, put an arm around me and guided me back towards the house. We walked in silence for a little bit, but I could tell she wanted to talk.

"So, I saw you and Nathan down by the beach together. Sitting really close. Closer than two friends would normally sit," she finally said, raising her eyebrows knowingly.

I knew she'd want to talk about Nate. Ever since we were little kids, she'd been certain that we were destined for each other.

Maybe that was one of the reasons I kept pushing him away.

"Whatever you think you saw, it didn't happen, okay? I just got back here. He still sees who I used to be. It's not the same."

"I know, sweetheart, but I see the way he looks at you."

"What way? He barely looks at me, and he only ever jokes around with me."

My voice sounded panicky even to my own ears. Did he really look at me? What did that mean? Maybe he thought the dramatic re-entry of his childhood friend into his life was an exciting distraction. He couldn't possibly like me—he just liked the thought of me. Who I used to be. He was spending time with me because he had to. But I liked spending time with him. And I'd just gotten here too. But that wasn't the same, was it?

"Arielle, sweetheart, I can see you overthinking it. Don't. Just feel it."

I lowered my head in defeat, knowing she was right but unwilling to admit it to myself.

Sensing my inner struggle, Mom quickly changed the subject, talking about how happy she was to be back at the beach and how lovely the weather was and how happy everyone seemed to be to see us. I just nodded, unable to answer for myself. The thought of what could have happened if we hadn't been interrupted on the beach filled my mind. Would Nathan really have kissed me? Or was all this just in my head?

"Hey, Jess, you can go in and turn on the fireplace! There's some cookies on the counter that we can snack on!"

How that woman had time to bake everything, throw a huge bonfire party, eat the amount of food that we did and still be hungry was beyond me.

I saw Nathan dust off his hands and offer an arm to his mother; she took it graciously and smiled up at him, nodding in our direction. He shook his head and laughed then looked up and saw me watching. I quickly whipped my head around and followed my mother inside. Thank goodness he'd finally found his shirt.

CHAPTER SIX

We stayed up even later, talking and laughing until my mother insisted it was time for her to turn in. Sarah protested for a second, before Mom gave her The Look. Before I could even say anything or make my escape with them, they hurried up the stairs, giggling like schoolgirls, leaving Nathan and I on opposite ends of the same couch. We smiled awkwardly. The silence stretched on for a minute, neither of us knowing quite what to do.

Just as I was about to feign exhaustion and head upstairs, Nathan leaned forward, rested his elbows on his knees, and looked over at me.

"You know, Ari, there's something I've been meaning to ask you for a long time."

His eyes had that twinkle in them again, and I had a feeling that whatever he was about to ask me, I wasn't going to like it. Or maybe I'd like it too much.

"And what would that be?"

As I spoke, he got up and sat down beside me. He wasn't touching me, but now he was much closer and could read my facial expressions well. Too well.

"The last time you guys came to visit, you did something weird before you left."

"Weird?" My voice betrayed me—I was strangely hurt.

I was pretty sure I knew what he was talking about, and it stung that he thought it was weird.

"No, no, I didn't mean weird. I mean, well, I don't know how to say it."

He looked flustered. Even when he was little, Nate had never looked flustered.

Then he grabbed my hand and pulled me up with him. "I'm going to show you."

His eyes never left mine. I followed him, in a trance, to the front porch. I remembered the moment he was talking about—the moment I'd fallen for him completely, in all my pre-teen glory.

"This was where it happened. It was a night like this one, and it was just you and me sitting here. You were telling me about the constellations, and I was trying so hard to be smooth, but you just laughed at all my attempts."

I nervously giggled at the memory. But he wasn't done yet.

He took both of my hands in his. "But what happened next is what I'm having a hard time with."

I gulped, not wanting to go there this soon. Hadn't I just arrived? This wasn't supposed to happen yet. Preferably we would never have this conversation, but we couldn't always get what we wanted.

"I asked you about next summer, and you got this look on your face. You told me that your mom was getting remarried, and that you wouldn't be coming back for a while. You tried to run away from me, but even then, I was stronger than you. After I gave you the most awkward hug of my life, you told me to hold still."

I turned away and pulled my hands free, unable to hear the story I'd played over time and time again in my mind. My head wished he would stop, but my heart was pounding, as if it couldn't take it if he did.

"You leaned in and kissed me before running into the house. But the next morning, you left without saying anything. Not even goodbye."

My eyes brimmed with tears, and I couldn't turn around. I felt him come up behind me and move the hair from my neck. The cool breeze hit my exposed skin, but what lit every nerve in my body on fire was the featherlight way his fingers brushed against my neck. I gasped. Just as quickly, his hands retreated, and I felt cold without them.

"It was the only way," I mumbled, trying my best to keep my voice level. I opened my mouth to say more, but the words wouldn't come. The fear of saying too much overpowered the fear of not saying enough.

There was a long pause. When Nathan spoke again, he sounded angry. "The only way? To what, break my heart?"

I turned around at the pain and anger that had flooded my best friend's voice.

"No, the only way to avoid an even worse heartbreak. I shouldn't have kissed you that night. I knew I wasn't going to see you again. And if I did, I knew it was never going to be the same. It was my fault. I got caught up in—in—"

Failing to find the words, I pushed past him and sat down on the porch, wrapping my arms around my knees. Sadness dominated my emotions. Taking a shaky breath, I tried to find some semblance of peace.

"Ari." His voice was much calmer as he slowly sat down next to me.

"It's easier to leave things calm and peaceful rather than make waves," I sighed, unsure what I was trying to say even as I said it.

Nathan put his head in his hands, moving his hair around in a way that told me he was irritated. And only Nathan could look irritated and cute at the same time.

"So you're telling me I should just let it be. Just pretend it never happened?"

I heard the pain in his voice. I was already putting myself in harm's way by even having this conversation. It became too much all at once, and I stood up—I couldn't take it anymore. Nathan's head jerked up at the same time.

"It was years ago, Nate. We were just dumb kids. If it helps you get over it, then yes—please forget about it."

I began to walk away, but a warm hand grasped my arm and pulled me back. Out of the corner of my eye, I saw my beautiful white sleeves now had soot and ash from the bonfire around the edges. I was dirty.

"Ari!"

My eyes fluttered open again. I hadn't even realized I'd closed them. Tears ran down my cheeks.

Everything was painfully clear. His eyes were big, trying to see my past. I turned, shutting him out. I was dirty. Soiled. He didn't deserve this.

I yanked my arm from his grasp and walked down the driveway. He followed me—silently. He didn't try to catch up; he didn't shout to try and stop me. All he did was follow as I walked, almost in a trance. The sand beneath my bare feet was soft, then it turned into hard gravel. I barely noticed.

I walked down the long winding road until it met the second road and merged into one, and I stopped. A fork in the road.

"Do you remember this place?" he asked softly, still behind me. Letting me feel what I needed to feel. Letting me have space while reassuring me he was there.

I nodded slowly, but I needed him to tell me again. I needed him to tell me everything would be okay.

He came up beside me. My legs began to shake, and he gently helped me sit on the road.

"Well, Ari, if I remember correctly, when you first came here, you didn't like me. At all. So, that first day, you tried to run away. You made it this far before I came running after you. My mom told me that if I didn't, I would lose my brand-new surfboard, so I came running."

I wiped a stray tear away as he laughed; I smiled at the memory of his little legs chasing after me.

"I told you to come back. I really didn't want to lose that surfboard. Do you remember that board?"

"Yeah, it was floral." I laughed at his expression.

"It was studly. Especially for a seven-year-old." He shook his head in mock disapproval.

My tears were finally slowing down.

"Anyway, you sat down, right here, and refused to come back with me. I asked you why you were being such a brat."

"And I asked you why you were being so rude." I smiled at the memory. That was the first time, but definitely not the last, that I'd taken Nathaniel Rentz by surprise. "We sat and talked for a while, and you were actually nice to me. For the first time."

He chuckled. "Yeah, well, being nice to you isn't always easy."

I shoved his shoulder—hard.

He just laughed and continued. "Every time you got upset, you'd come to this spot."

"This was where all my decisions were made. I remember, in all my six-year-old wisdom, I told you that this was the spot where I'd decide 'what direction I wanted my life to take me.'" My voice was still tight with emotion, but I gave him a weak chuckle. "Who would have known that it would become my runaway spot for everything?"

"When you lost a surfing comp for the first time, when your mom got mad at you for mouthing off, when I got mad at you for being a brat." He smiled at the old memories.

"Hey, this spot wasn't just for when I was being spoiled."

"Oh, definitely not. It was also for when your mom started dating again, when you won first place at one of the big comps, when my dad left, when you got into that prestigious summer program for science."

We sat in silence for a minute—then I reached over and grabbed his hand. He didn't turn and look at me in shock. He didn't gasp in surprise. He just squeezed my hand, as if he'd been waiting for me to come to him all along.

Eventually, we stood up, and I leaned against Nathan's arm for support as we made our way back to the house. We didn't talk, but it wasn't awkward. It was a comfortable silence, and I was just happy Nathan seemed to have let it go and we were back to being friends again. He didn't drop my hand until we were back inside the house. I didn't mind.

Nathan dropped me off at my room, but as I reached for the handle, he reached for it too. His hand touched mine, and I hesitated before pulling it back. Holding hands before had felt different, like when we were kids. But now, standing outside of my door with Nathan towering over me, it was obvious we weren't kids anymore.

"Sorry," I mumbled. Why was I so awkward around him?

He just smiled and reached his hand out again. It felt like a decision.

I smiled hesitantly up at him before placing my hand tentatively in his. He pulled me towards him, until our faces were inches apart and I could see the flecks of gold in his bright-blue eyes. The moment was charged, filled with everything that had been spoken and everything that had been left unsaid. He took a deep breath—but I couldn't do this. Not yet.

"Nathan, we can't do this. Whatever this is. We haven't seen each other for years. I—I just want my best friend back."

I saw the hurt in his eyes, the flash of fight, then the resignation. I hated hurting him, but I just needed time. Time to learn to trust people again. "It's too much."

"If that's really what you want, I'll respect that." Then he pushed a strand of my hair back behind my ear and leaned in close.

My head told me to back away, to keep my distance. Whatever he was about to do, I couldn't let him. But my heart immobilized me—his touch made it pound and want him even more.

Then, slowly, as if trying not to scare me away, he leaned in and kissed my cheek.

"What was that?" I asked in shock. Friends didn't do that.

He just smiled and stepped back. I felt cold again and had to stop myself from stepping towards him.

"Just a reminder."

"A reminder? Of what?"

"Of what we will be. You know, when you come to your senses." And then he winked.

He turned and walked down the hall to his room. "Night, Ari."

"Goodnight, Nate."

I quickly opened my door and stepped inside before the night could get any stranger, then flopped onto my bed, not even bothering to crawl under the pale-yellow comforter.

After tossing and turning, replaying every moment from that day, I finally drifted into a restless sleep.

CHAPTER SEVEN

The next morning, I woke to a light knocking on my door.

"Hey, Ari?" The door opened and Sarah stuck her head in.

I rubbed my eyes, lifting my head up and twisting around slightly to see her before groaning and putting it back down.

She walked in and sat next to me on the bed. She put a hand on my shoulder, attempting to get my attention, but sleep was calling my name again.

"Ari, did you sleep in your clothes last night?" She stood up and walked over to the closet.

That comment finally got my attention. Had I? I sat up, rubbing my eyes as I did so, and looked down at myself. Sure enough, I was still in my white shirt and denim pants.

"I guess so. I don't really remember; I was so exhausted."

She opened the closet and began to shuffle around. "Well I can't really blame you, after the day you had yesterday."

I knew she was talking about the road trip but all I could think about was Nathan. I leaned over to check the clock on the white nightstand next to the window.

It was only six thirty. I groaned again and flopped backwards onto the still perfectly made bed.

"Aunt Sarah, I love you, but why are you waking me up at six thirty in the morning?" I grumbled, staring up at the ceiling.

"Because, Ari girl," she said as a bright pink swimsuit landed on my face. "It's tradition, and I want to fully initiate my surf goddess back into the beach."

As I sat up, I held up the revoltingly neon thing between my two fingers, keeping it as far away from me as possible. "Okay, there's no way I'm wearing this."

She put her hands on her hips. "Honey, it was my favorite bathing suit when I was your age!"

I slowly pushed myself off the bed and laid the thing on her shoulder as I walked past her to the closet.

"Well, it just so happens that I'm not an eighties fashion icon like yourself." I smiled at her and began pushing through the inordinate amount of swimwear hanging in the closet. A yawn escaped as I spoke. "Still hanging your bathing suits, I see."

Sarah walked over and took a seat on the bed, laughing as she did so.

"Well of course. You know, I read somewhere that the most important items of clothing you own will be found hanging up, in the prime real estate of your closet."

"Which is why the only things hanging in your closet are bathing suits and sundresses?"

"Yep." She cocked her head to the side as my gaze landed on an elegant black-and-white one-piece. "That one is beautiful. Not very fun though."

"I guess that's me then." I smiled as I took the swimsuit off the hanger. "Not very fun."

Sarah frowned and came up behind me, resting her chin on my shoulder and looking at the one-piece. "Just because something is simple doesn't mean you can't make it fun. And just because it's simple doesn't mean it isn't absolutely beautiful."

"But why do things that used to be so simple become so complicated?"

She turned me around and looked at me, as if trying to read my mind. She had blue eyes, just like Nathan, twinkling with energy, but hers were lighter, like the sky. Nathan's were like the ocean. But they pierced the soul and twinkled with joy just the same.

"This isn't just about a bathing suit, is it?"

I shook my head slowly, and Sarah sighed.

I'm sure she didn't want to deal with this. I didn't want to deal with this. But I knew the mental and physical toll that suppressing emotions took on me. I wanted to be better.

She turned and took a seat on the bed again, patting the spot next to her. I slowly sat beside her, clenching the black-and-white fabric in my hands. Keeping my head turned away from her, I examined the carpet closely. There was the paint stain from the first time I'd tried to paint Nathan's nails—with wall paint. It had taken a full hour to convince him to let me try, and I'd insisted the paint would wash off right after.

It took fifteen minutes for our moms to find us, and two weeks for every speck of bright-yellow paint to finally come off. Nate was mad for the first three days but then promptly forgave me when I showed him my secret hideout.

I frowned. Why had it become so complicated?

"Sweetheart, is this moodiness about what happened before you came here?"

I glanced up at her, not surprised that was her first assumption. "Mom told you."

She nodded slowly. "She was scared. I can tell that you both are."

I didn't say anything. I felt nonsensical. Immature. Childish. Wrapped up in a boy when the world was crashing down around me.

"I am. We are. We lived that way for so long, it's hard to just go on and act like it never happened. It's just, I don't want to think about it. Whenever I do, I—I just—" My hands started to sweat, and my mind started to black out again. I stood up quickly, and the black faded.

"Hey, hey, you're okay." Sarah stood up with me and hugged me close. "Breathe—breathe."

I breathed deeply. I was better than this. I wouldn't let him control my life.

"I'm fine. I won't allow this to run my life. But I can't go through a single day without these attacks taking over. And it's frustrating, and annoying, and I can't tell Nathan what's really going on."

"Hey, you're the strongest girl I know, Arielle. This is a tough situation, and definitely one I prayed would never happen to good people like you and your momma. But you both have strong souls—and even stronger wills." She squeezed my shoulders and turned my chin so I was facing her. "You'll be just fine. And you can tell Nate in your own time, but I suggest doing it before he thinks you're pushing him away for other reasons."

I nodded, understanding her concern for her son.

She gave me a quick kiss on the forehead then looked past my shoulder at the windowsill. I followed her gaze, which had settled on the shell fragments I'd emptied from my pockets before I'd crawled into bed. It hadn't escaped my notice that she'd kept the old mason jar full of shell pieces I'd collected when I was little.

Without saying a word, she reached out and touched one of the shells, then turned and headed towards the door. As she opened it, I sat back on the bed, deep in thought.

"Come on, Ari. Are we going to go surfing today or not?"

Nathan's voice jolted me out of my thoughts. I looked up to find Sarah was gone and her son had replaced her in the doorway.

"I don't think I'm ready for surfing yet, Nate."

I couldn't risk it. I couldn't act like everything was normal when it wasn't. The pull to the ocean was strong, and being so close to the waves was making my hands ache for a board and my body yearn to be in the beautiful curl of a crystal-blue wave. But I wasn't ready. And until these blackouts were under control, I couldn't trust myself.

"I can see your mind working." Nathan stepped fully into the room, seeing too much and too little all at once. His eyes darted to the bathing suit I still had clenched in my hand. He didn't say anything, just came and sat down next to me.

We stayed that way for a long minute. I could feel his gaze on me; he was clearly waiting for me to give in to the urge to surf.

"It's just not going to happen today, Nate. I'm sorry to disappoint you—I just can't." I turned to look at him, but he dropped his gaze before I could figure out what was going on in his head.

"Are you going to tell me what's going on with you?"

There was a tightness in his voice that felt like a stab to my heart. I wanted to tell him. I wanted to just tell him everything that had happened, and how much I needed him. But all I could feel was this grimy, dirty sensation. He wouldn't see me as his precious Arielle anymore, and that would truly break me.

"I will, I promise. I just need time."

He ran a hand through his hair and let out a deep breath.

"Can you give me that? Please?"

He smiled warily, as if he didn't really believe I would ever tell him. I hated that every conversation we were having was about me pushing him away. Thankfully, Nate was on the same wavelength.

"I'm done with all this gloomy serious talk. I have an idea." He grabbed my hand and pulled me along behind him.

We ran down the stairs, past a stunned Sarah and Mom in the kitchen, and out to the beach.

"Nate, wait, where are we going? Nate!" I called, and then a thought popped into my head. "The caves?"

"The best substitute for a sunrise on the water is watching a sunrise from the caves." We shared a smile. "Wanna race?"

I laughed as he dropped my hand and took off in a sprint, still running towards the pier. And I took off after him.

There was a spot just past the pier where we would go to hide to get focused before a comp or just to be alone together. The caves—our secret hideout.

We joked around like that for a while, one of us sprinting ahead of the other and then switching as we laughed. Finally, I pulled ahead. We'd slowed to a brisk walk at that point, but the competition felt the same.

My eyes were set on the cliffs, and I was so lost in my thoughts that I didn't see Nathan come up behind me.

He wrapped his arms around my waist, picking me up like I was nothing, then spun me around, his laughter mixing with mine as we twirled in the sand until we collapsed in a dizzy heap, sprawled inches away from each other. I was breathless with laughter, trying to regain some composure as I pushed myself up to my feet. Nathan stayed on his back, laughing and reaching to pull me back down, but I was too fast, too determined to make him chase me this time.

As soon as I started running away, I knew he would catch me—sooner rather than later. Sure enough, he grabbed my hand a few seconds later, and I let him.

I slowed down to walk beside him, letting the tingles spread through my palm, racing their way to every point of my body. I wanted so badly to be close to him again, like when we were kids. I could trust him with anything. This was Nathan.

"Idea," he said randomly. We were still a little way from the caves.

"No," I answered quickly.

He let go of my hand and crossed his arms in mock protest as we kept talking.

I tried to hide my disappointment at the loss of his hand by rolling my eyes. "Okay, what?"

"What if we played twenty questions?"

"Um. Why?"

"Yesterday you said that I didn't know who you were now. That you've changed. So prove it."

He sounded so proud of himself, I couldn't help but smile.

"Okay. Shoot," I said, letting his joy wash over me.

"Favorite color?" he asked with a grin.

"Easy. Blue. Yours?"

"Green. Easy. Favorite food?"

"Mexican obviously. You?"

"Mexican obviously," he repeated, grinning. Then his eyes got all twinkly again. "Opinion on *Grey's Anatomy*?"

"You already know this! You know I can't stand how inaccurate most of the medical stuff is," I huffed, already fired up. He knew this was my debate of choice. "And how they all sleep with each other? Good drama, fine, but I can't do it!"

"Okay, okay, crazy, calm down." He laughed again and gave me a look.

I couldn't figure out what the softness in his eyes meant. "What?"

"Nothing," he muttered, looking away.

I nudged him with my shoulder.

"I was right."

"Right about what? Not about *Grey's Anatomy*."

"No, about the fact that I still know you. Even if you don't believe it." He laughed.

I gave him a questioning look, and he stopped in his tracks. I stopped too, nervously meeting those determined eyes head on as he spoke.

"Let me guess, you still get your Mexican food regardless of the dish with sour cream, guac, and salsa all on the side. You have to skip the part where Mufasa dies in *The Lion King* because it makes you cry, but you won't skip the part where he tells Simba to remember who he is and you cry anyway. You tuck your hair behind your ears when you get nervous, and despite not wanting to surf, for some reason the ocean keeps you calm."

I gaped.

He pointed a finger at me, started walking backwards towards the pier, and smirked. "The parts I don't know, I'm sure I'll learn about. Because if you think we're not gonna spend this summer together, you're lying to yourself."

With that, he spun back around and picked up the pace. That was just fine. I was speechless. And terrified.

That word rebounded in my head over and over.

Together.

I knew he didn't mean it like it sounded, but that didn't stop me from picturing what that would look like. What we would look like.

In a comfortable silence, we made it to the caves. There were two small ones, sandwiching the huge entrance to our hiding spot. The rock, dark and glistening with mist from the night before, arched up in a wide opening. The light only reached a few feet in, especially this early in the morning, but sitting right under the ledge, it felt as though you could see the whole world. From that spot, the ocean stretched for miles, and the sun rose over the horizon in brilliant, golden rays.

I got to the entrance first, and in my haste to climb up the small incline to the opening, I lost my footing. My sandal slipped off my foot, but Nathan grabbed it quickly before regripping the rock with it in his hand. His other hand grasped my waist to steady me. After sharply catching my breath, I rolled my eyes. Of course he'd have super-fast reflexes.

"Whoa, you good, Ari?"

"Yeah, just don't want to miss the sunrise," I mumbled as I pulled myself into the cave and sat with my feet hanging off the ledge. My heart pounded from just those two seconds of contact. This was bad.

Nate pulled himself up next to me, and no sooner had he sat down than he was leaning over, attempting to put my sandal back on my foot.

"Hey, do I look like Cinderella to you?" I let him fit my sandal back on my foot as he shook his head.

"I would call you my princess if I thought you'd let me." He laughed again as he got a hard shove to the shoulder. "Ow, okay, I take it back."

"Good. I'm no princess." I kept a forward gaze, but I felt his eyes move to me. "And I didn't say that to get a sympathetic response or for you to contradict me either."

"That's good, because I don't feel bad for you and I'm not gonna contradict you. You're right, you are no princess."

Now it was his turn to keep his gaze set on the horizon as I stared at him in shock.

After a moment, he turned to meet my questioning gaze with a soft smile. "You're way too tough. Plus, I don't think you need anyone to save you. You've got it."

I was surprised by his sweet words. In the past week, I'd never felt weaker or more useless. Hearing Nate tell me who he knew I was… it was too much. I turned away so he couldn't see the tears starting to swell in my eyes. I felt a hand on my shoulder, but I couldn't bring myself to turn to him.

"Hey, hey, hey. Ari, let me help you. Maybe if you weren't so stubborn and would just let me in—"

"You think I want to keep shutting you out?" I cried, whipping around.

Nathan's eyes grew wide, and his hand moved back as if he was surrendering.

"Do you think it's fun for me to keep pushing you away when all I want is for you to make me feel better?"

"Then let me help you, Ari. Stop pushing me away."

"You want to help me? Stop pushing *me*. Why can't we just have fun like we used to?" I was infuriated. Royally pissed off. He would never see me the same. Why couldn't he accept that I was protecting him? "You just said we'd have fun this summer. Why do you insist on being so serious all the time? Wasn't the whole reason we came to the caves so we wouldn't have this same conversation? You said you'd give me time."

"Why can't you just trust me?" Now his voice was filled with anger. It had been a long time since I'd heard actual pain and frustration in his tone, and it broke through all my walls, piercing right into my heart.

I felt the tears fighting to come out, and I couldn't bring myself to look at him anymore. Pushing myself from the ledge, I slid back down the sand and started walking somewhere, anywhere else.

I heard him call my name, but I didn't listen. I didn't look back. I just kept walking. *Just. Keep. Walking.*

I missed the sunrise.

CHAPTER EIGHT

I wandered for a few hours, walking further down the beach than I'd ever gone alone before. Miles and miles of warm sand passed under my bare feet, while I held my sandals in my hands. I wanted to feel something other than pain and fear. I didn't want to hurt anymore. The silence was almost worse, allowing every hard, awful moment to replay over and over again in my head. Finally, I closed my eyes to try and shut it all out.

"Ow," a small voice cried out as something thudded against my legs.

My eyes shot open, but the voice had come from the ground. I looked down to see a little girl sprawled at my feet.

"Watch where you're going, lady!"

I must have been so out of it that I'd run into her. Feeling awful, I bent down to help her up. She had bleached-blonde hair and light green eyes, just like me. She looked up at me for an explanation, her face scrunched in anticipation.

"I'm so sorry. Here, let me help you."

But before I could even touch her, she sprang up.

"I don't need help." She dusted the sand off her scrawny little legs.

I smiled—she had spunk.

"How old are you, kid?" I asked gently, still squatting in

front of her so our gazes were level. She peered into my eyes, and I could feel that trust didn't come easily to her.

"I'm almost seven. My name is Lexi by the way." She stuck out a hand, and I laughed at her adult mannerisms.

"Well, Lexi, you're very mature for your age," I said as I shook her hand.

Letting go, I stood back up and looked around. I didn't recognize my surroundings. The beach continued to stretch on, and there were several families sitting out with coolers and big umbrellas, even though it couldn't be later than ten in the morning. But this was a part of the beach I hadn't ventured to in my younger days. A pier reached out into the water, like a hand grasping towards the horizon, but it didn't have a Ferris wheel like the one at Avila Beach.

I looked down at the little girl, who surprisingly hadn't run off yet. "Hey, do you know where we are right now?"

"This is the beach. That is the ocean," she said matter-of-factly, pointing to each thing as she listed them.

"I know that much, Lexi. Which beach is this? Do you know the name?"

She looked puzzled for a second then started jumping up and down. "Yes! It's called Pirate's Cove Beach!"

I smiled at her enthusiasm. I hadn't wandered too far—only a few miles from Sarah's house.

"Thank you."

She smiled back at me then just as quickly turned and ran into the ocean, the waves knocking her back as she giggled joyfully. I watched her for a moment, remembering a time when I'd been just like her. Innocent—and happy just because.

I walked a little further, to the pier, as the beach started filling up with more families and the water became crowded with surfers—experienced, beginners, and in between.

Walking along the boardwalk, I kept my gaze lowered to avoid any eye contact. Couples lined the edges, arms looped around each other as if letting go would mean they weren't together anymore.

I felt more alone than ever, and my mind went to Nate more than it should have. The longing in my chest I'd felt the night before, staring at the horizon and wanting someone to look at me and understand, returned—stronger than I'd ever felt it.

Suddenly, I felt a hand on my wrist. Fear flooded my body, and I whipped around, pulling my arm away and stumbling backwards. I blinked, relief flooding my body as I recognized who the hand belonged to. He wasn't who I'd expected.

"Whoa, sorry to scare you, Ari."

Kyle's big smile made me less anxious, but my heart was still racing. His puppy-dog eyes seemed concerned, but his face was trying to put me at ease. My mother had used the same face on me more times than I could count.

"Kyle. You can't just sneak up on people like that." I wrapped my arms around my waist, trying to protect myself.

"Sorry, I just saw you walking and thought I'd come say hi. I thought you'd be with Nate today. He was really excited for you to be back." His smile lessened and turned more into a disconcerted frown.

I gave him a small smile before looking out towards the caves. "Uh, yeah, I was with Nathan. It's not as easy to be back as I'm guessing he thought it would be."

Kyle laughed at that. "It never is when there's a pretty girl involved. Especially with Nate."

I turned my head to the side, questioning him. What was that supposed to mean?

He just laughed again, ignoring my curious look. "Anyway, what are you doing here? Isn't there a pier right next to Sarah's place?"

"I could ask you the same thing." It came out a little snappier than I'd intended.

"Well, grumpy, it just so happens that my mom lives over on this side of town while my dad lives over by Sarah's place."

Almost too quick to notice, a flash of pain traveled across his face. I felt awful for my grumpiness—he was just trying to be nice, even though we'd barely talked at Sarah's party.

"I'm sorry."

He just shrugged. "You didn't have anything to do with my dad cheating on my mom. Don't apologize for it."

I gave him a weak smile. He was kind—I could see why Nathan was friends with him.

I opened my mouth to ask him why he wasn't surfing, when his phone rang. He pulled it out of his pocket, squinting to see the caller ID in the bright sunlight, then glanced up at me.

"One sec. It's your boy." He answered the phone and turned slightly away from me. "Nate! What's up?"

I couldn't face him. Not yet.

Without thinking, I brushed past Kyle and started walking back towards the entrance to the pier. He didn't follow. I walked in a daze, quickly heading back in the direction I'd come from until I found myself back at the caves. Footprints covered the ground, too many to be just mine and Nate's.

Suddenly, I thought of how worried my poor mother must be. In my pain and stubbornness, I hadn't even thought of what she must be thinking. I was so selfish. So unbelievably selfish. Luckily, I knew she wouldn't risk calling the cops. He could be tracking that. He could find us from that.

I walked quickly down the beach, hardly even looking up until I reached Sarah's sliding glass door. I heard voices speaking anxiously on the other side. I took a deep breath before sliding the door open and stepping through.

"Well where else could she have gone? She's a smart girl—she wouldn't go far," Sarah was saying pragmatically, a comforting hand on my mother's shoulder as she supported herself against the counter, her head down in despair. Sitting on the couch, with his head between his hands, was Nathan.

I looked at him for a moment, not knowing whether to step fully inside or retreat while they still hadn't noticed me. I remembered the little girl from the beach, Lexi—how innocent she was. How she reminded me of myself. How Nate made me feel that pure and wanted again. Thoughts of his contagious laugh and warm smile pushed me through the door, which I slid shut behind me.

As soon as the door clicked into place, his head shot up. He stood up quickly, accidentally pushing back the couch as he did. My eyes never left his as we stood in suspense, each waiting for the other to move first. We never got to see who would have caved, since my mother ran and wrapped me in a tight embrace. Peering over her shoulder, I saw Nathan sit back down and resume his original position.

"Sweetheart, where were you?" Mom asked as she pulled back and grabbed my face in her hands. "We were worried sick when Nathan told us you'd run off."

"I'm sorry, Mom. I just needed some time to think."

She pulled me close again, and I felt her body begin to shake with sobs.

"Honey, do you realize what I thought happened?" she cried.

I knew exactly. She thought he'd found me. She thought he'd taken me.

"I know, I know. I'm so sorry. It won't happen again."

I stroked her hair until her tears subsided. She leaned against me, breathing heavily. I felt how weak she was, and I knew the emotions were finally catching up to her, the way they were with me. We'd ignored them for too long.

"Hey, Mom, look at me. I'm safe, and I'm so sorry I scared you. Why don't you go rest for a while?"

She hesitated a minute, looking over my body one more time as if confirming to herself I was truly okay. Finally, she gave me a feeble nod.

I looped my arm around her shoulder to support as much of her body weight as possible then steered her towards the stairs.

Out the corner of my eye, I saw Sarah sit next to Nathan and put a comforting arm around him. She glanced up at me, giving me a small smile and an encouraging nod. I returned her smile and continued to guide my fragile mother up to her room. We made the trek in silence, her labored breathing our only communication.

Once I got her into bed and pulled up the covers, her hand grasped mine, and I took a seat on the edge of the bed, grasping her hand right back. Her eyes began to close as I stroked her hair, but just when I was sure she was asleep, she muttered something.

"What was that, Mom?" I whispered, leaning forward to hear her more clearly.

"Darling, I don't want your fears and pain to keep you from living." Her eyes remained closed, like they were too heavy to open.

"I know. I'm trying. It's just—I can't—"

Her eyes fluttered open, and she squeezed my hand hard. "Baby girl, I know how hard this is. Just try. For me, please just try to let someone else in. I know why you left. I know you needed to sort through your thoughts. I know it was your way of pushing Nate away. You bottle it all up, and then you explode. I want you to let it go, and let people in. Please, baby."

"Okay. I'm going to try. You and me, Mom," I whispered.

"Always, always." She paused. "And now, you can have you and him. You just have to choose it."

And with that, she closed her eyes and released my hand. Her words hit me in the chest, solid and irrepressible. My dear mom, who'd sacrificed the most and had the most to be angry and hurt about, was telling me to let him in. To not let my emotions push people away.

To make a choice of my own.

Leaning forward, I placed a kiss on her forehead—gentle, so as not to wake her—then left the room, shutting the door softly behind me.

CHAPTER NINE

Halfway down the stairs, I knew what I wanted to say to Nathan. I wanted to tell him everything. I needed him to know why this was so hard for me. To know how I really felt about him. But could I find the words? And the courage?

When I walked into the kitchen, Sarah was pulling a tray of cookies out of the oven. She was a stress baker. And an excited baker. Really whenever she had a strong emotion or something big was happening, she baked. Her stress baking was never as good as her excited baking though, and sure enough, when she turned, I could see the cookies on the tray were slightly burned.

She glanced at me before turning to shut the oven door and set the cookies down.

"Sarah, I'm so sorry for all the craziness I've caused. I didn't mean to disrupt your summer." I lowered my head, suddenly very aware of my blindness to the consequences of my actions.

I felt a hand on my shoulder and looked up, surprised that I hadn't heard her move.

She looked down into my eyes, and I noticed her hair was frizzier than usual. Her eyes had little wrinkles at the sides, and her smile was less joyful than I remembered. But despite the obvious toll that time had taken on my beloved Auntie Sarah, I could feel how good her heart still was.

"My darling Ari girl, you and your mother are always, always welcome here. The fact that you're even able to compose yourself after what happened—well it's more than I'd be able to do."

She pulled me close for a second before releasing her hold entirely and going back to the slightly overdone cookies. "If I did have one complaint, however, it would be how oblivious you are to my son's feelings."

My jaw dropped. Sarah had always been blunt, but had she really just come out and said *that*? Was I really about to have this conversation with his mother?

"Well, I mean, we're just friends—" I stumbled over my words and Sarah cut me off as she laughed at me. Not with me. Definitely at me.

"My girl, you've never been 'just friends.' Even when you were little, Nate always had a crush on you. What I still can't tell is how you feel." She spoke with the confidence she always carried, moving the cookies over to the cooling rack as she did.

"I mean, I just got back," I began as I moved closer to where she stood. "I've only been here for a day and we haven't seen each other in years. How does he even know who I am anymore?"

I knew exactly how I felt, but I couldn't feel this strongly. Not this soon. Not after all this time and definitely not after everything that had happened. It was too much.

Sarah just sighed. "Something tells me you know he knows exactly who you are. And that's not what I asked."

I looked out the kitchen window towards the ocean. There was so much more to consider here than just my feelings.

"I think you already know how I feel," I whispered. My heart pounded so loud I was sure the whole world could hear it.

She turned towards me with her spatula still in her hand, her eyes open wide, and her smile grew. She pointed out towards the shoreline. "Then why are you still here talking to me? Go tell him. Or," she quickly added, seeing the fear on my face, "if that's a little too much for now, just give him a sign. Something to show him he has some hope."

I nodded slowly, turned from the kitchen with my mom's words ringing in my ears, and hesitantly made my way out of the house towards the ocean.

Let him in.

He was standing, hands in his pockets, facing the horizon. As I approached, I thought of all the things I wanted to say. I had no idea where to start.

He turned as I came up beside him, but his face was full of confusion as he turned back towards the ocean.

I stood by him for several minutes, simply listening to the waves as they came in and out. I'd thought he might yell at me for running off, chastise me for acting like a child. I wanted him to say something. I sighed, knowing that, for once, I would have to make the first move.

"Nate, I'm sorry I ran off. That wasn't fair to you—or Sarah or my mom. And I'm sorry I pushed you away again. You didn't deserve that—well, you don't deserve the way I've been treating you at all. You're my best friend, and I should start treating you like it," I said quickly, the words tumbling from my mouth so quickly they were almost running together.

He barely moved. Just kept looking at the horizon, as if it held all the answers. Finally, he turned towards me. There was a familiar glint in his eye.

"Which time are you referring to?" he asked with a boyish smirk.

I rolled my eyes at his question, puzzled but also feeling the tightness in my chest begin to loosen at his joking tone. "What?"

"Well, if I remember correctly, you've pushed me away a minimum of three times in the past day. And sorry to break it to ya, Ari, but you've been running from your problems ever since I've known you." He smiled as I laughed again. "Which time specifically are you referring to? Because I'd love to hear you recount some of the better ones."

"Would apologizing for all of them work? Every time I've made you run after me because I'm a sad, sappy, emotional girl." I watched him as I spoke, trying to make him feel my sincerity.

He blew out a big breath, leaning back on his heels before he met my eyes again. "That's a lot of times. You know"—he dropped to a whisper, leaning close—"I bet I would win the 'Chasing Arielle' Olympics at this point."

"Oh well, you know there are several people contending for that gold medal. I hear it's a pretty tight race these days," I teased, pushing his shoulder as he laughed too.

"Yeah, I think one of them might be my buddy Kyle."

He roared with laughter at my shocked expression. "He just messaged me. When he saw you at the pier this morning, he apparently assumed we weren't getting along, romantically speaking, and was very excited to invite you to a big party he's throwing Friday night."

"Well, um, I mean—"

Nathan cut me off with his chuckles. He was always good at being lighthearted about my discomfort.

"Imagine his surprise when I told him you would be there, as *my* date."

This time, I knew not to let my shock show. Even though my face wanted to show everything I was feeling, I didn't want him to see my eagerness to do anything and everything with him.

"And what makes you think I'll be there as your date and not Kyle's?" I replied, trying my best to seem unaffected.

He smiled down at the sand, as if there was a joke hidden there.

"Arielle, you didn't even know Kyle was interested. And you, the mighty Ari, just apologized for pushing me away." He shuffled closer. "I'd say my chances are a little higher than his."

"That's assuming you ask me before he does." Now it was my turn to giggle at his shocked expression. "It seems, my old friend, that you've forgotten an important part of going on a date with someone. Did I teach you nothing when we were kids?"

He wrapped his arms around me tight then and spun me around. I held on, knowing that things between us were changing.

When he finally stopped spinning me, he let my feet touch the ground but kept his arms wrapped around my waist. I glanced up to find our faces were only inches apart. Breathing heavily, I looked at his flushed cheeks and suddenly got very nervous. This was Nathan, but this was Nathan all grown up. He wasn't a little boy anymore.

I broke the spell when my nerves took over, quickly stepping back and staring at the ground.

"What was that for?" I asked hesitantly.

"You laughed and joked more in that five minutes than you have the entire time since you've gotten here." His smile was so genuine, so beautiful. "It was like having the old Ari back for a minute, and I just couldn't help myself."

"Um, well." He'd thrown me completely off guard. The moment was too sweet. I couldn't taint it. Not with the story I needed to tell him.

It took another breezy grin from him to solidify my decision. There would be a better time to tell him everything. Not when we'd just reclaimed the lightness I craved from him.

"What time will you pick me up?"

His smile grew wider. "How does seven sound?" he said confidently.

I returned his infectious smile with a small, nervous one of my own. "Don't be late."

"Wouldn't dream of it."

CHAPTER TEN

"Mom?" I called as I made my way down the stairs the next morning. I'd barely rolled out of bed, throwing on an old band T-shirt of Sarah's and my trusty jean shorts, before making my way downstairs. Even though Sarah had made it perfectly clear I was welcome to anything of hers, I still felt weird just raiding her closet.

When I got to the bottom of the steps, I turned towards the kitchen, where bright sunlight filtered through the glass door and windows. The crash of waves against the shore met my ears like a soothing song, and I closed my eyes, taking a moment to listen to the familiar sound of the ocean.

Something about the ocean spoke to my soul and settled me. I wasn't sure if it was the memories of summers spent in the water, or the way it was constant yet was always changing. The tide would come in, and then it would go back out. Waves would crash against the shore. Then it would be calm. The sand was always shifting and changing. You could go to the same spot every day, and you could count on it being different. And yet, the sun always set on the horizon.

What did I crave more? Consistency or change? I felt stuck between wanting both so much it hurt. All I wanted was to be normal, whatever that was. To live in peace, yet I couldn't see what that looked like. But I knew I'd never be happy being stuck. I'd had enough of that to last a lifetime.

"Ari? Is that you?" Sarah's voice reached me, and my eyes slowly fluttered back open. She stepped into the living-room space, closing the sliding glass door behind her. She had a towel and a book with her, sunglasses perched on her head. I glanced at the oven clock—it read 10:33.

Wow, I really had slept in.

"Good morning, Auntie." I gave her a small smile. "Is my mom up yet?"

Sarah's face changed, but she covered it quickly with a smile. I suddenly felt off-kilter. I knew she hadn't felt well yesterday, but was something else wrong?

"Is she okay?" I asked frantically, taking a step towards Sarah.

She immediately came to me, setting her free hand on my shoulder and looking into my eyes with warmth and concern. "Oh, yes, Ari girl. She's just stressed, and I think she needed more rest than she realized." She gave me a small wink. "Sleep and otherwise."

Still worried, I glanced back up the stairs. Sarah dropped her hand from my shoulder and made her way into the kitchen, dropping her stuff on the counter as she went.

"Okay, sweet girl, I have an idea. You wanna get out of this house with me?"

Did I? I wasn't sure where Nate was. It was on the tip of my tongue to ask, but I didn't want to seem overeager. Even though I really, really wanted to see him. And was also terrified of ever facing him again.

There were a lot of feelings to sort through. So I gave Sarah a small nod. We could do some feelings sorting later. Much later.

After a quick stop at a bakery for some muffins and lemonades, we pulled up to a strip mall. I glanced over at Sarah, who was excitedly eyeing the surf shop as she took a sip of her lemonade.

"Shopping?" I asked.

"I don't know every detail, Ari girl, but I know that you have one pair of jean shorts and one shirt that I know you've had since middle school. Personally, I think you look killer in my clothes." She unclipped her seat belt and started opening the door with keys in hand. "But I also know you like to have things of your own. You and your momma are the same that way."

And with that, she was out of the car. I scrambled to undo my seat belt then opened my door and stepped into the parking lot.

"But I don't—" Sighing, I shut my door before coming to meet her behind the car. "Sarah, I don't have any money. We couldn't take much. So I don't—I can't—"

"Arielle Hansen." Sarah's voice was stern. Her gaze was intense as she bore into me with those piercing blues. She and her son had that in common—they could spear you with just a look. "I've missed six years of celebrating your birthday and you just graduated high school. This is a gift. So no more talk of 'can't.' Let me do this. Please."

She reached for my hand and gave it a light squeeze. I looked down at my old, ratty flip-flops. I hadn't thought about clothes in forever. Finally meeting her gaze again, I gave her a smile and a nod.

"Yeah?" she asked.

I nodded again.

"Alright, girl, let's do it!"

She linked arms with me and started chatting about an article she'd read concerning current wardrobe essentials as we wandered into the first shop. It was a thrift shop, full of every style and fashion you could think of. The saleswoman called out, welcoming us in. Sarah called back, but I was focused on the rows and rows of clothes. There were so many.

Sarah steered me towards a rack of denim then released my arm and began shifting through some jeans. I just stood there, arms at my sides, overwhelmed by all the options. Where did I even start?

"Come on, Ari. Just pick whatever's calling to you," Sarah called back to me from over her shoulder. "I'm not sure if you like those jean shorts, but they're way cute! Maybe we could grab a few more pairs, if you want?"

I hesitated, edging closer to the racks. There were a ton of different styles, and there were tons of jean shorts. There were some with flower patterns stitched into the back pockets, some with little diamonds along the belt loop, others with excessively frayed edges. But after flipping through a few pairs, I still wasn't sure.

"I'm not sure. I do like my jean shorts," I said, unsure of what to do. Shopping definitely didn't come naturally to me. "I can pick any of them? How do you know which one is the right one to pick?"

"Ari girl, you pick whatever makes you feel like you," she said softly, pausing her search to glance over at me.

What felt like me? I'd never been one of those girls with a distinct style. Or really any type of style. I wore what was bought for me. I'd never put much thought into it before. My mom had a distinct style. She wore flowy skirts, flared jeans, and loose shirts. She had a casual, free type of vibe.

Everything about Sarah screamed "I live at the beach." From her wild hair and sun-kissed skin, to her brightly colored sundresses and tan sandals. They both knew who they were, and it showed.

"What if I don't know who that is?" I whispered, looking down at the floor.

Sarah crossed the space in two seconds, taking hold of my shoulders again. She peered down at me, taking her time before answering. Then she tilted my chin up with her knuckles and gave me that intense gaze once again.

"You listen to this old lady, Ari girl. It's so absolutely normal for someone your age to still be figuring out who she is. You're not sure who you are? Then take your best guess. You do whatever feels right. That goes for clothes, boys, school, decisions, all of it. You keep guessing until it clicks. Then sometimes it unclicks and it changes and you start guessing again." She took a deep breath, her gaze fixed on mine. "Until one day, you feel comfortable in your own skin. You don't let anybody tell you what to feel or how to be, because it will never be right. Only you can tell you what you feel—who you are and who you want to be. Got it?"

"Got it." My voice was unconvincing, but I did my best to hear her words and let them sink in. Sarah had this way of reaching into all the doubts of my soul and making me see the possibilities. She always had. "You're pretty wise, you know that?"

A small smile crossed her face as she released me, grabbing a few jean shorts and holding them up for my inspection. I nodded in approval as she started talking again.

"Wise? Not sure if I'd go that far, girl. I've just had a life full of unchosen adventure." She grinned mischievously as she pointed to a stand of old T-shirts a few racks over. "Let's see what they have over there. Maybe something will catch your eye."

As we wandered over and started making our way through the T-shirt rack, Sarah's words kept playing in my head.

"Auntie Sarah?"

"Hm?" She held up a bright-red shirt that looked like it would barely cover the top of my chest. I quickly shook my head. No way.

"Did you ever have to guess? Was there ever a time you didn't know who you were?" I asked, flipping mindlessly through a few shirts to give my hands something to do.

Sarah took a second to consider my question as she put the red scrap of fabric back, pausing her scan of the racks to glance over at me.

"Did I ever tell you the story of how Nate was born?" she said finally, giving me a small smile.

"I don't think so."

"Well, you see, he was sort of an accident. The best accident ever but definitely not planned." She sighed. "Nate's dad and I were high-school sweethearts who broke up when we went to college. When we saw each other years later, home for the summer, we got a little carried away one night. And nine months later, Nate was born."

"I had no idea. I barely remember Nate's dad."

"Oh, that's definitely for the best. His family was the type that attended catered events at the country club with champagne flutes. All stuffy suits and fake friends. Total backstabbers."

"I can't even imagine you living like that." I shook my head as I chuckled, imagining Sarah being fake. Or attending a country-club event. Ever. It just didn't fit.

"Yeah, me neither. Needless to say, my thrifted sundresses and love of bonfires and grungy beach days was a disappointment to his parents the first time around. But when I rolled up to their porch, broke and pregnant with their grandson, they went into makeover mode." She laughed a bit, but I could hear the pain in it. "The point is, they tried so hard to fit me into their world. The stuffy clothes, the events, the connections. They even politely asked if I could stop listening to my music in their house."

"They didn't!" I exclaimed.

"They did. I can't blame them for lacking good taste in music. My hair was always straightened, and even now I cringe at the amount of heat that was applied to my curls during that time." She touched a hand to them, shuddering at the thought. "Anyway, the point of this story is that trying so hard to fit into their world was miserable. It took away every scrap of who I thought I was and turned me into someone I didn't recognize, let alone felt comfortable being. After Nate was born, I took one look at his sweet, innocent face and knew I never wanted him to be a part of that. I wanted him to always be able to choose who he wanted to be."

"Is that why—" I stopped myself before I could ask a really, really insensitive question.

"Yes, my dear girl. That's part of the many reasons his dad left. After Nate was born, I started guessing. Choosing different paths until things clicked." She gestured to herself playfully. "I finally was comfortable in my own skin again. And I wasn't willing to change for other people. Your momma helped a lot with that, being such an amazing friend when I was struggling and constantly fighting with Nate's dad. But, sweet Ari, that's life, isn't it? We do the best we can—and keep going until it all feels right within us."

She reached out to hold my cheek for a second, and we shared a smile. I was raised by such strong women. My mom and Sarah. There was such heartache and such love all wrapped up in their free spirits. I loved it so much. I never wanted to take it for granted.

"Anyway, enough about me! Anything here catching your eye?" she asked, resuming her search through the shirt rack.

I turned my attention back to the rack, flipping through a few shirts until my gaze landed on an oversized shirt with a graphic on the front. The colors were faded, but it was the Olympic rings.

I bet I would win the "Chasing Arielle" Olympics at this point.

I smiled, my thoughts wandering back to our conversation on the beach. I glanced at the next shirt. This one was another oversized graphic tee, but this one had a sunset graphic on it. I kept searching and came up with three more oversized T-shirts with graphics on them. They each made me smile.

"I'm sensing a theme here. Oversized shirts and jean shorts?" Sarah asked when I showed her my haul. "I love it."

"That's my guess for now. I'm gonna go with it," I said, shrugging. We shared a smile before heading to the fitting rooms at the back.

After another few hours of shopping around, our stomachs were growling, and our arms were loaded with bags. They were mostly full of oversized T-shirts, jean shorts, flip-flops and sneakers. And I couldn't keep the excited smile from my face. Because they were mine.

When we pulled into the driveway, starving, Mom was sitting on one of the rocking chairs on the porch. She had a glass of lemonade in her hand and her smile was directed towards the side of the house. Following her gaze as Sarah parked, I saw Nate on a ladder, fixing something on the roof.

He smiled down as my mom said something, and that smile sent a buzz through my whole body. When he smiled, he got these little lines near his eyes. I watched his muscles flex as he reached up to do something. My breath hitched at the sight of him. I had to admit, he was pretty good-looking.

Okay, he was hot. Undeniably.

"Hey, Nate hon, could you come help us with these bags?" Sarah shouted as we both exited the car.

"Oh, Aunt Sarah, it's okay—I can carry them up," I protested.

But Nate was already down the ladder, making his way over to us. He gave his mom a quick side hug, pulling her close as his gaze drifted to me.

"Sure thing, Ma."

Our eyes met, and heat flushed my cheeks. He just had this way of looking at me. It was everything and not enough all at once.

Ari, chill out. Jeez.

I barely heard Sarah give him instructions to take them up to my room as he grabbed all of the bags, obviously planning to do it in one trip. He shot me a quick smile before disappearing into the house.

"Thank you!" I shouted when I finally realized I hadn't said it out loud. I heard something muffled called back as I took a seat on the porch near my mom.

Sarah placed a quick kiss on my head before giving Mom a quick hug. "How are you feeling, Jess?"

"Oh, so much better. Seems like you guys had a busy morning?"

"Well, you know how I feel about girls having their own clothes. We'll have to go when you're feeling up to it." She smiled at both of us. There was no condescension. No judgment. She just was happy to do it.

"Thank you so much for today. It meant a lot," I choked out, emotion suddenly overtaking me. She gave me another knowing smile.

Mom laid her hand on Sarah's arm. "Really, Sarah, thank you so much. We appreciate it more than you could ever know." There were tears in my mom's eyes too.

Sarah just nodded. "You both are my family. A few clothes and a place in our home is the least I can do. Truly." Wiping at her eyes quickly, she snapped her energetic smile back into place. "Alrighty, I'm going to fix up a late lunch. It'll be leftovers, so I'll just pull it out of the fridge, and we can do some good old reheating."

And with that, she stepped back into the house.

Mom glanced down at me, still looking exhausted but smiling. "Did you have fun?" she asked.

"Yeah," I answered genuinely. "It was nice to spend some time with Sarah again. And just feel normal."

We shared a smile. It was something we both felt. This weight was slowly lifting from us, and we were enjoying the lightness it left behind.

Without warning, rain started falling in sheets. I glanced up at the bright sunlight in confusion. There were no rain clouds in sight. But there was definitely rain.

"Ari!" my mom gasped. "It's a sunshower! You know what that means!"

I giggled. "It is tradition."

"That it is, sweetheart. Let's do it!"

She jumped out of her seat, grabbed my hands, and pulled me into the rain. We started laughing as we began spinning in a circle—faster and faster until we couldn't keep hold of each other anymore. The rain kept falling, plastering our hair to our faces and making our clothes cling in all the wrong places. But it didn't matter.

This was our tradition. Anytime it rained, we danced in it. And when it was a sunshower, we would spin. We hadn't done it in years. But the sunlight was making each raindrop glisten, creating pure magic all around us.

As our hands lost their grip, I threw my arms out and spun solo. Finally, out of breath and exploding with laughter, I stumbled to a stop and glanced at the house to find someone leaning against one of the posts on the porch, watching us.

Nate's blue eyes met mine, and I couldn't look away. Pushing my wet hair out of my face, I just stared at him, and as he smiled at me, I felt something I hadn't felt in a long time. It was fleeting, only for a moment. But it was there.

I felt safe.

CHAPTER ELEVEN

The rest of our week fell into a pattern. I would sleep in, normally until ten. Nate and Sarah would have been up for hours, but my mom normally woke up around the same time as me. Sarah and Nate would join us for the biggest brunch of all time, then we'd hit the beach. I was so excited to wear my new clothes, for once feeling like I was dressing for me.

Sometimes we would walk around; sometimes we went to the pier. My mom normally got tired in the afternoon, so we'd head back, and she would lie down for a nap. Nate had something planned every day. One day, we met up with Kyle and Luke at the arcade. I wasn't very good at any of the games, but it was entertaining enough to watch them get so excited about beating literal ten-year-olds' high scores. Luke even cracked a smile.

Another day we watched movies until dinner. It was so easy to be with Nate. He didn't try to hold my hand or put his arm around me when we watched movies—as much as I secretly wanted him to. We shared popcorn, but he kept his distance. And I was grateful. It made me feel like he really was my friend, regardless of all the other feelings we had. And each night, I tossed and turned before finally drifting away into a fitful sleep.

"Ari?"

My eyes stayed shut. My bed was so cozy. There was no way it was morning. Nope, I'd just go right back to sleep.

"Ari!"

This time someone shook my shoulder. What the—? I jolted up, smacking my head on something really, really hard.

"Ow! What—" I exclaimed before a hand clamped over my mouth. I startled at the contact as blue eyes met mine. We both held a hand to our heads, and Nate groaned as he rubbed his.

"Jeez, Ari, you've got a seriously thick skull," he whispered, grimacing in pain.

I rolled my eyes at him, seeing as his other hand was still clasped tightly over my mouth. Glancing down at it, I raised my eyebrows expectantly at him. He just raised his right back.

"Will you keep it down if I move my hand?"

I rolled my eyes again at his serious tone and nodded. He eyed me skeptically but finally removed his hand, and I pretended to be disgusted, wiping my mouth with the back of my hand.

I should be an actress.

"Okay, drama queen."

"Nate, are you gonna tell me why you needed to wake me up at"—I glanced at the clock on my nightstand as I whispered—"eleven thirty at night?"

His eyes twinkled, and I knew I was in trouble. I was already going to say yes.

"Wanna go stargazing?"

The cool summer breeze rustled my hair, and I could taste the salt on my tongue as we lay on a blanket in the sand, staring up at the sky. Our bodies were in different directions, our heads next to each other with our feet pointing opposite ways. The stars were so beautiful. Small, iridescent dots lighting up the sky. It was crazy to think that something so small and seemingly so insignificant could be so breathtaking. So powerful. But maybe that was just the power of perception. If you took a star at face value, it was just a twinkling light in the night sky when really it was so much more. It was a powerful, burning ball thousands of light years away. And it was beautiful.

"Red or orange?"

"For a wedding dress?"

"Yes."

"Nate, no. I know you're thinking neon red or orange. Neither would suit my skin color. If it was pastel, maybe."

"Wait, we didn't specify if it was for your wedding or not. Unless it's a bright-red wedding dress! Oh that's edgy, Ari."

I reached my arm up and shoved his head to the side as he chuckled.

"I believe you said, and I quote, 'Ari, so I'm just spitballing, but what wedding-dress color would you prefer to wear?'" I laughed at my impression of his deep voice.

"I don't sound like that!" he protested.

I giggled. "That's exactly what you sound like!"

He made another sound of protest, and we both erupted into laughter.

A comfortable silence settled over us for a few moments as we took in the stars.

"Ari?"

"Yeah?"

"What was high school like for you?"

I stiffened. Images flashed through my head, but I shut my eyes. I shut them out. Taking a deep breath, I compartmentalized. Half-truths. Those were my safety.

"I mean, it was just school for me. I wasn't really super social. I had one or two girls I hung out with at lunch. But I was really just focused on my classes." I shrugged, trying to appear nonchalant. "What was it like for you?"

He took a minute before he answered. It was weird talking to him without looking at him. But I kept my focus on the stars, knowing how close it would put my face to his if I turned.

"It was fine. I mean, I had Kyle and Luke. We were all on the surf team together, so that was always fun. But honestly, most of the time, I struggled."

I felt him shrug next to me.

"School didn't come super easy to me. Girls were sometimes too much drama to deal with. I don't know—it was fine, I guess."

He fell silent after that. A few thoughts were crossing my mind. I sat up, needing to sort through them. There was something about the dark night and starry sky that made me feel like I could share them. I felt Nate sit up too, and I turned to face him. Folding my legs underneath me, I locked eyes with him as he waited expectantly for me to speak.

"Do you ever wonder what the point is?" I asked.

"Of high school?" He tilted his head in confusion.

"No. Yes. I mean, what's the point of all of it?"

"Ari." He smiled mischievously. "Are you asking me what I think the meaning of life is?"

"Maybe?" I grinned sheepishly. "Have you ever thought about it?"

The breeze picked up at that moment, sending my hair across my face. Nate pushed it behind my ear, just like he had at the bonfire. The rush I felt was instant. Intoxicating. It made me catch my breath. Especially when he hesitated to pull away. But he did, moving back and glancing down as he considered my question.

"Yeah. A lot actually," he said softly. "School was a struggle, but honestly life as a whole was a struggle for those few years. Mostly because I was trying to be the man of the house while also trying to figure out what was so wrong with me that my own dad didn't want to be a part of my life anymore."

My heart broke for him.

"I didn't make good decisions a lot of the time. Spent a lot of time with people who didn't really care about me, only that I was a good time and I was down for whatever." He took a deep breath, glancing down at his hands as they fidgeted in his lap. "I made a lot of mistakes, Ari. I have so many regrets. But when I finally pulled my head up, I felt like I could see things clearer."

"So you figured it out?" I asked softly. Maybe he had. Maybe he knew the meaning of life.

"No, not even close." He laughed softly, glancing up at me. "But you know what I did figure out?"

"What?'

"That it's okay not to know."

I stared at him as I let that sink in. He reached out, lacing his fingers through mine before he started speaking again.

"I don't know what the purpose is sometimes, but I do know what makes me happy. I know who the important people in my life are, and for now that's enough. That's what I focus on."

He gripped my hand tighter as he smiled. His skin felt so warm, his hand so big around my small one. Looking down at our intertwined hands, I contemplated his words.

"And what is it that makes you happy?" I asked softly.

Fingers softly guided my chin up, so I was level with Nate's face. It suddenly struck me how close we were. I could feel his breath on my lips as he spoke.

"A lot of things. My mom. She's always given me every-thing. My friends. Surfing. Hobbies. Good food. The stars. The ocean." He paused, and he focused those eyes on me again as he spoke. "Being with you. You've always been a happy part of my life, Ari."

I swallowed; I knew Nate wouldn't lie. He was always so genuine. So honest.

"What makes you happy, Ari?" he whispered, still holding my hand. His fingers kept my chin in place.

"I don't really know," I whispered back. "But I want to figure it out."

I saw a quick flash of something like disappointment in his eyes, but it was gone as soon as it was there. He let his hand drop from my face and shifted back. My heart ached at the space between us. But my words were true—I knew what used to make me happy, but I just wasn't sure anymore. I wasn't sure of any of it. But looking at Nate, at the kindness in his eyes, I wanted to find out.

"Then let's figure it out," Nate said, smiling. Then he held his free hand up in the air. "I, Nathaniel Rentz, hereby swear that I will help you, Arielle Hansen, discover what makes you happy this summer. I shall do this by showing you all the fun to be had in Avila Beach during your stay, so we can discover the true happiness of the real Arielle Hansen. Deal?"

He moved his hand to the space between us, offering it to me. I shyly let go of his other hand—which I'd still been holding—and took his extended one. We shook once, and I smiled.

"Deal."

A loud noise jolted me from the deep sleep I'd been in. I shifted my body, but I was tucked up against something hard and unmoving. I shifted again, and this time I felt something rodlike supporting my legs and back.

"Shh, Ari, we're almost there."

I knew that voice. One more shift, and it clicked—I was being carried. Every part of my body was exhausted. Sighing, I snuggled even more into a very firm chest. In my sleepy state, it wouldn't register until the morning that the strong arms carrying me were Nate's.

I felt my body being lowered, and a soft mattress welcomed me into its warm embrace. I snuggled instantly into the soft pillow as a blanket covered my legs and torso. A warm hand stroked my cheek.

"Goodnight, Ari. I hope you liked the stars." A soft whisper. But I'd already faded back into the darkness.

I did. I loved the stars.

And I really liked the boy who'd showed them to me.

CHAPTER TWELVE

Friday finally came.

Nate had some plans with Luke and Kyle to hit up an old surf shop across town and catch some waves, so I hung back with Sarah and Mom that afternoon and helped bake cookies and cook dinner. Nate and I had barely spoken to each other all day. I was nervous. This was my first date.

When the day started to wind down at last, dinner was tense. Mom didn't come down until halfway through, and just seeing the dark circles under her eyes made me angry at *him*. But watching her try to smile and sing along to the radio, I knew I had to stay strong. For her.

Nathan was acting funny—he didn't seem as confident as he had the rest of the week. I nudged his foot under the table, but he barely met my eyes long enough for me to shoot him a questioning look. And then he ignored it, lowered his head again and went back to poking around at his food. Nate was a human garbage disposal, so that alone was concerning.

Sarah was the only one talking, mostly to herself, about the glorious surf today and the inordinate number of cookies she and I had baked. I was so lost in thought I almost missed her train of thought, which had somehow traveled from cookies to relationships.

"Speaking of stress, since you two are heading off to that

party tonight, what did Ari say that helped you kiss and make up on Monday?"

At that, I jolted, and Nathan's fork hit the plate with a loud clunk as his head shot up.

"Metaphorically speaking of course." She smiled at my mother. Mom turned expectantly to the two of us. Those troublemakers.

I stared at my plate as heat rushed to my face, thinking it might dissuade them from asking more questions. Apparently dodging the embarrassing question and getting flushed was some sort of unfortunate code.

"Wait, you guys kissed?" Mom exclaimed excitedly.

Sarah clapped her hands together, and Nathan started stuttering and telling her to stop.

"We didn't," I said quickly.

Nathan finally met my eyes, and I smiled hesitantly. Sarah had said to give him a sign, but except for the night with the stars, we'd been very strictly friends all week. "I mean, I don't kiss until after the first date."

With that, I stood up, grabbed my plate, and left the table. Had I just said that? It had all come out in an awkward rush, not the calm, confident way it had sounded in my head.

Squeals of excitement and the loud scrape of a chair against the floor followed me as I put my dishes in the sink. A plate landed in the sink almost immediately after mine.

I turned into Nathan, almost bumping into his chest before taking a step back. He opened his mouth to say something, but I didn't want to start a conversation that neither of us knew how to finish. Not when I was already so on edge.

"See you at seven," I said quickly, brushing past him and practically running up the stairs to my room.

I'd barely closed the door behind me when my mom came in. Her face was happy, and her eyes were alive with excitement. It almost made the darkness under her eyes seem lighter.

Almost.

"Oh, honey, let's make you look even more beautiful than you already are."

"Mom, it's really not a big deal. We're just going to his friend's party together."

She just shook her head at me.

"Really, we've gone places together tons of times. With some of these friends. It's super casual. No big deal. Why is everyone so excited now that we put a fancy title on going to a party?"

"Because, my dear, stubborn child, this means that you're no longer keeping Nathan at a distance. You're letting him in." I felt my lips tug up in a small smile at her happiness, which she didn't even see since she'd already rushed over to the closet.

I looked down, realizing my usual choice of clothing was so plain. Why did he even like me? I wasn't the prettiest, the smartest, the funniest. I was just me. A girl with a normal body, a little scrawny in some places but not model skinny by any means, average features, and a tendency to run away when things got hard. I sat down on the bed in despair. Maybe I couldn't do this.

An article of clothing was thrown at me, and I barely caught it before it hit me in the face.

"Stop overthinking, Arielle. That's an order." She turned back to the closet and continued to search through some of Sarah's more extravagant clothing for the perfect outfit. "You and Nathan have always been great together. Just have fun."

"I'm going to give it my best—it's just scary," I sighed. "There's no going back to being just friends after this. I can feel it. And we're really good at being friends."

Mom turned and threw all the clothes she'd gathered down on the bed then grabbed my hands and pulled me up. Grasping my hands tightly, she looked deep into my eyes.

"My darling, you deserve the world. And I'm not just saying that because you're my beautiful daughter. You have a capacity to love that not many people have." She sighed. "You have this wall you've built up to protect yourself, and I know part of that is my fault—"

"Mom, no. You didn't know who he really was."

"I saw the signs and ignored them. Let me at least take responsibility for that. But it goes deeper than that for you, even back to when we lost your dad. We both need to realize that. But… *him*. I need to take some responsibility for my actions."

I nodded—she wasn't going to let it go until she felt like she'd taken it upon herself.

"The point I was trying to make was that you can't live your life in fear. Sweetheart, you have the world at your fingertips. If you always hide behind this fear of what could go wrong, you're never going to be happy. Let yourself fall fully into something, and for once, don't worry about what could go wrong. Don't keep it on the surface. Don't overanalyze it—just let it happen."

We stood in silence for a minute, tears welling up in both of our eyes.

"Wow, Mom. You should be a motivational speaker or something."

She just laughed and pushed my hair out of my face. "I've been trying to tell you, honey. You didn't get those smarts from thin air."

We both started giggling lightly, and I hugged her tight. Her arms felt warm and protecting, like only my mother's could.

"I love you, Mom."

"I love you too, sweetheart." She finally let go and held me at arm's length. "Now let's make this surfer boy fall head over heels, shall we?"

It was 6:58, and Mom was trying to explain why I should wear lip gloss as opposed to just chapstick when Sarah poked her head through the door.

"Okay, Jess, I think it's time we start watching that rom-com we've been dying to see and leave these two to themselves."

"You're right. It's time to set the young ones free," she said wistfully, then turned and placed a kiss on my forehead. "Good luck, honey. And remember, let yourself have fun, okay?"

"Thanks, Mom. I think I'm ready."

"I'm glad you are, because Nate is still freaking out." Sarah laughed—and was still giggling as my mom pushed past her and pulled her out of the room, giving me an encouraging smile before closing the door.

Once the door was closed, I walked to the small mirror that hung next to the window, between the closet doors and the bed. In the reflection, I saw a girl with straight blonde hair and wide green eyes. She looked peaceful. She looked happy. I smiled. For the first time in years, I felt normal. I thought back to lying under the stars with Nate. Things had been changing between us when I left six years ago, and we'd picked up right where we left off.

My palms were sweating, because a sweet boy I liked way too much would be knocking on my door any minute to take me to a very awkward beach party that was probably going to be boring, with cringy music and a bunch of people who'd probably be full of themselves.

And I couldn't help but smile to express my excitement.

My mom had picked out a pair of jean shorts and a black lace shirt for me. She said it was cute yet casual, perfect for a first date, and made it feel more special than if I'd worn one of my oversized tees. She hadn't, however, been able to talk me into the tan wedges she'd dug out of Sarah's closet.

As I slipped on my trusty flip-flops, I heard a noise outside my door. Thinking maybe my nerves were making me imagine things, I continued looking in the mirror.

Then I heard it again.

I ran a hand through my hair and pulled open the door. There stood Nate, pacing in front of my door in a light-blue shirt, his curls still wet from a shower. His head was bent over his watch, and it shot up when he realized I'd opened the door.

"Ari! What are you doing?" His eyes were wide with fear, as if I'd just broken a law or walked through a crime scene.

"Um, coming to meet you for our date."

"No, no, no."

"No?"

He pointed at his watch, as if that would somehow explain his mystifying behavior. I just raised an eyebrow.

"Arielle, there are still nineteen seconds until seven o'clock."

I shrugged, still not understanding.

He let out a big sigh. "I told you I'd be on time, but it's first date rule number one to never be early."

"Okay, Nate, it's not a big deal. Let's just go—"

He held up a hand to stop me as I tried to step into the hall.

"No way, missy. You go back inside and shut the door until I officially pick you up."

"Oh my gosh," I sighed dramatically. "You're really going to make me go back for five seconds?"

"Um, yeah—seven and half actually." He waved his hand at me, like an old lady shooing a pesky child back into line. "We're doing this right."

I groaned as I shut the door, but an uncontrollable smile spread across my face as soon as I was safely out of view. It was sweet. Really sweet. For a moment, I felt all flustered. This was really happening—there was no turning back. Whatever Nate was to me now, he couldn't be just a friend.

A few seconds later there was a brisk knock on the door. Deciding to play along, I opened it a crack so only half of my face was visible.

"Can I help you?"

Now it was Nathan's turn to be exasperated. "Ari, can you please open the door?"

"Hmm, I don't know."

He threw his hands up in the air, but the smile in his eyes let me know he was enjoying our little joke.

"Is it seven yet?"

He checked his watch, and in a movement so quick I barely had time to react, he pushed the door wide open, grabbed my hand, and pulled me into the hallway so fast I stumbled into him. Using my one free hand, and Nate's chest, I got my balance while he just smiled down at me.

"Jeez, Nate, what was that?" The last part of my sentence dropped into a whisper and lost its sassy quality as I looked up and realized just how close our faces were. He just smiled his dazzling smile and let me sink deeper into his blue eyes before he finally whispered.

"It's 7:01. You almost made me late to pick you up."

I just smiled. "You're really taking this first date seriously, aren't you?"

He opened his mouth but shut it just as quickly. A barely visible shake of his head followed.

"What?"

He still didn't answer. He wouldn't even meet my eyes. It seemed the endless confidence of my date had faded.

Surprisingly, I still had a little left. One hand still firmly in Nathan's, I used the other to gently nudge his chin up, forcing him to look at me.

The tension in the air was so thick, it almost felt like I was drowning in it. But every time I felt my head dipping beneath the surface, I remembered whose beautiful ocean-blue eyes I was drowning in.

"Nate," I whispered. "What is it?"

Keeping his hand in mine, he moved the other up to cup my cheek. I closed my eyes at his warm touch, letting myself lean into his hand. This was Nate's magic. For years, I'd never let my guard down in front of anyone—always alert, always waiting for the other shoe to drop. But now, with my heart going a million miles a minute, I knew I was safe. Because Nate held my hand. It was dangerous, but I couldn't quite bring myself to care.

I let my eyes flutter open and found he was still looking at me. I couldn't figure out why he was looking at me like he couldn't bear to look away. He shuffled closer, until our faces were so close they were almost touching. His eyes closed slowly, and he began to lean in.

"We need pictures!"

The voice that normally brought such comfort and joy to my heart now sounded like nails on a chalkboard.

We sprang apart a mere second before Sarah appeared at the top of the stairs, holding an old digital camera that she still insisted on using. I kept my face down, too embarrassed to make eye contact with Nathan. Would he really have kissed me? I was surprised by how much I wanted him to.

"Mom, it's really okay."

The traces of frustration in his voice forced me to look at him. His jawline was pulled taut, but from his profile I could only get a glimpse of his feelings. He was definitely annoyed.

For some strange reason, him being upset at not getting to kiss me made me really, really happy.

"Thanks, Sarah, but I think we're going to be late."

Without waiting for a response from either of them, I started walking down the stairs. I heard Nate following behind me. Once I'd made it safely to the kitchen, he ran in front of me to slide open the screen door. I realized we never used the front door, unless one of us was running away or leaving for good. It was just the way this house worked.

"Thanks for getting us out of there," he said as I walked past him. He stepped out behind me and closing the door then came and stood awkwardly next to me.

"No problem." I gave him a small smile.

The silence felt like it stretched forever.

Finally, Nathan gestured towards the endless expansion of beach. "Shall we?"

"We do have a deal."

He grinned. "Let's have some fun."

CHAPTER THIRTEEN

It took us fifteen minutes of uneasy joking and pitiful attempts at playful banter to get to the party. It was awkward. The almost kiss was haunting me, and I found myself overthinking more than usual. And I was always overthinking things.

When we arrived, there were already tons of people there. Music blared from two large speakers set up around the bonfire, despite it being a fairly warm summer night. Tons of guys and girls were standing in groups talking, dancing, and there were even some boys throwing a football back and forth closer to the waves.

We both looked at each other apprehensively before Nate nodded towards the masses of people, signaling for us to move forward. I hated this awkwardness that had settled between us after our—well, whatever it was.

We'd barely moved towards the crowd when a loud voice shouted over the music and the chatter.

"Nate!" Kyle, with a cup in his hand, dodged a group of dancing girls to make his way over to us.

"Hey, man, what's up?"

I took an uneasy step back as they did the classic bro handshake-hug thing that's apparently a universal way for boys to greet each other.

"Oh you know, just throwing a massive party." His eyes

shifted over to me. "Ari! Glad you found your way here! You had Nate scared out of his mind. He finally picks a girl, and he has no idea if she's gonna show!" Kyle broke out into laughter.

I offered a small giggle, glancing at Nate just in time to see him roll his eyes. This was the perfect opportunity to break the awkward tension, and I wanted nothing more. So I clung to the last thing Kyle said.

"Wait, Kyle, what do you mean 'finally picks a girl'?"

Nate's head snapped to attention at my question. Maybe that was the wrong thing to joke about.

"Well, Miss Ari, your boy Nate has gone through all of Avila High's finest—"

Before he could get any more out, Nate pulled me to him and covered my ears with his hands. Our laughter was uncontrollable, and the heaviness that had been sitting on my chest finally lifted.

"Okay, and this is when I take the pretty girl away from my loudmouth friend." Nate released my ears and placed his hand on the small of my back, guiding me towards the make-shift dance floor. Kyle bumped fists with him as we made our way through the crowd, shouting out some encouragement for Nate.

Kyle had been kind of weird around us earlier in the week, giving some substance to Nate's claim that he was interested in me, but any lingering feelings had definitely faded now. He seemed genuinely happy for us. He was a good guy.

We'd reached the group that was apparently dancing, and I was unsure of what to do. When I'd "danced" with Kyle at Sarah's bonfire, I'd mostly laughed while he'd done the sprinkler and shopping cart to Blink 182 songs. This wasn't quite the same.

I'd never gone to parties in high school, not even a single school dance. And I definitely didn't know how to dance with a guy. Especially if that guy was Nate—the only guy I'd ever liked.

Seeing my obvious confusion, Nate reached out and grabbed my hand. I smiled hesitantly up at him as we began to "dance"—or just jump around extremely close to a ton of other people—to the EDM remixes Kyle was blasting on the beach.

After a while, the music finally chilled out and so did the partiers. A lot of people had coupled off and started wandering to various parts of the beach where they thought they could be alone. Surprisingly, Luke and a pretty brunette had started walking towards the water a little while ago. Luke had given us a small smirk before turning and following the girl.

Others were gathered around in various small groups, talking and laughing. Nate and I had danced for a while, never straying farther than a couple feet away from each other. Being so close to him made my heart pound. We ended up sitting with Kyle, some of their surfer friends, and their girlfriends.

Everyone was laughing and joking, telling surf stories and joking about each other's luck with the ladies. At some point, Nate had put his arm around me, pulling me close. It felt so natural. So easy to just be with him. I leaned into him and laid my head on his shoulder. My heart raced, and I fought to keep my face from showing every little thing I was feeling. And there were a lot of feelings.

"Hey," Nate whispered in my ear. "What are your plans tomorrow?"

I shuddered at how close he was to me. But I had to play it off.

Moving my head slightly off his shoulder so I could see his face, I gave him my best attempt at a carefree smile. "Oh you know, I have a very busy schedule of sleeping in and looking at the ocean. Why?"

"Well, um, if you have the time in your busy schedule, I might have a surfing competition." He nervously scratched the back of his head with the hand that wasn't resting on my shoulder. "Would you, uh, would you want to come? It's the last one I signed up for with the school surf team."

I just looked at him for a second. His eyes nervously searched mine. It had been so long since I'd been to a surfing competition. There would be so many people. It would be loud. But one look at the nervous boy in front of me and I knew I'd be there.

"I can probably make that work," I whispered. "If you want me there, I'll be there."

"I want you there." He didn't even hesitate.

Loud laughter erupted around us, and I smiled to myself as I glanced away from Nate and tried to focus on the conversation happening around us as my heart filled to bursting. As I laid my head back on his shoulder, everything felt right in the world.

Despite his constant protests, Kyle began very theatrically telling the story of how Nate had attempted to do a 360 in a surfing competition and had only succeeded in making three other surfers wipe out with him. But in the middle of the story, there was a shout from behind us. I lifted my head to see what was going on, just as Nate let out an exasperated sigh. I still couldn't see anything.

"What is it?" I asked, straining to see over Nate's broad shoulders.

"Wow, Arielle and Nate. Finally together. I guess we always saw that one coming, huh?"

Nate sprang to his feet to face Johnny and his friends. I scrambled to get up, in case things escalated again. I had a bad feeling they would.

"What are you doing here?" Nate's hand curled into fists, but Johnny's grin only widened.

"Just here for a good party—and the pretty girls of course." His gaze slid to me, that same glint in his eyes I'd seen the last time we'd met. Things were escalating faster than I'd expected.

I grabbed Nate's arm, begging him with my eyes not to fight. "Let's just go, okay?"

"Hey, Arielle, why don't you hang out with us for a while? We can show you a good time." Johnny stepped closer to me.

I suddenly felt as though every inch of my skin needed to be covered. I knew his type of guy. I was all too familiar with it. And it wasn't good.

"She's with me, Johnny. Now leave," Nate practically growled.

Johnny held his hands up mockingly, as if he hadn't intended to get that exact reaction.

Then he looked at me again. "The Arielle from when we were kids would never have let a spoiled little surfer brat speak for her like that," he sneered, baiting me. "What happened to you? Lost all that bravery? What made you so weak?"

His words pierced my soul. Things had happened to me. Things that made me hide. Things that made me push people away. Things that were real. Things I could never forget. Suddenly I was angry. It was because of a man like Johnny that I couldn't let an amazing guy like Nate in. It was because of him that I was always scared. It was because of him I blacked out. It was because of him I was broken. Because of him I was lost in every single way.

I met Johnny's gaze, but all I could see was *him*.

Without even thinking, I stepped forward and curled my fist.

And I swung.

CHAPTER FOURTEEN

I turned away and started walking as I heard Johnny stumble backwards and let out a scream of pain.

My steps were happening in slow motion. Fuzziness swirled in my head, and I knew my hand should have been throbbing with pain by now. But it wasn't.

It just felt numb. Everything was numb. There was a ringing in my ears, and my face was flushed with heat. I kept going. It was all numb. All I felt was numb. Numb, numb, numb. Then more feelings.

Lost. Stupid. Incompetent. Weak. Broken.

Broken, broken, broken.

Suddenly, I felt a hand wrap around my wrist. In a panic, I swung again, but Nate caught my fist just before it hit his face.

"Whoa, Ari, it's just me."

I looked around slowly. Everything had been such a blur, I hadn't realized how far I'd walked from the party. I could barely see the fire in the distance. Definitely couldn't hear the music. My ears felt like they'd popped.

Nate's hands reached up, cradling my face and forcing me to look straight at him. We stood like that for a moment, and I waited for him to ask what was wrong with me. To let go and refuse to touch me ever again. I'd gone insane, and if I were him, I would have walked away long before that moment. With his eyes peering deep into mine, his strong hands gently cradling my face, he asked me the question my heart was screaming to answer truthfully.

"Are you okay?"

I burst into tears. Everything—all the fear, hate, sadness, and longing—bubbled up and became so intense I couldn't keep it in anymore.

He didn't jerk back in shock; didn't turn around and walk away. He dropped his hands from my face, pulled me forward, and held me as I sobbed.

"I'm sorry," I whispered after the sobs finally subsided. I had no idea how long we'd been standing there, but long enough that his shirt was soaked with my tears.

He shook his head against my shoulder, still holding me tight. "Don't ever apologize for being hurt," he said forcefully. "Ever."

We finally pulled apart, but only far enough to see each other's faces. He kept his arms looped around my waist, and I kept my hands around the back of his neck. I wasn't sure at what point they'd worked their way up there.

"Can I at least apologize for being an ugly crier?" I tried to joke, to cover up my embarrassment. I reached a hand to cover my face, waiting for him to tease me. Instead, he grabbed my hand and pulled it away from my face.

"You know what," he said softly as he reached up and gently wiped away an errant tear, "I think you're even more beautiful when you cry."

I blinked. Once. Twice. My heart thumped so loudly in my chest I'm sure he could hear it.

"You've never called me beautiful before." The words escaped before I could stop them, tumbling out of me in an awe-filled whisper.

His eyes widened only for a second before he put his face very close to mine. I could see the sincerity in his eyes before he spoke.

"I should have."

Before I knew what was happening, Nate's lips pressed against mine.

My body melted, and it was only his embrace that kept me from falling at his feet. I'd never felt electricity like that. The millions of thoughts that had been racing through my mind seconds before disappeared and there was only him. Only his arms around me and his lips on mine. It was a sweet, light kiss. But it held everything.

Too soon, he pulled away. My eyes fluttered open to find him staring at me intensely. I hadn't been ready for it to end.

"Is something wrong?" I asked.

He laughed softly at my question, then leaned down and pressed a quick kiss against my lips. "No, absolutely nothing is wrong right now."

He grinned, and I smiled shyly up at him.

"I just want to take things slow with you. I know something big happened, and I know you'll tell me when you're ready. I just don't want to mess this up. I don't want you to leave again."

Happiness flooded my entire body. This sweet, gentle boy was capturing my heart more and more with every passing moment.

"Nate." I reached up, cupping his cheek with my hand. "I can't believe someone with such a big, beautiful heart would choose me."

I couldn't let fear hold me back anymore. Not from Nate. I needed to let myself fall. Or at least try, even though I was scared out of my mind. The way he was looking at me was something I'd never thought I could have.

"Ari, I've chosen you every day since we were seven and you told me if I didn't teach you to surf, you would never talk to me again."

I bowed my head as I laughed softly.

Almost as if he couldn't bear to not look at me, he lifted my chin with his fingers. "Even then, I knew I couldn't choose anyone else."

With tears streaming down my face, I pulled his lips to mine again. This time was different. Our first kiss had been gentle, sweet and tender—this one was full of emotions and driven by feelings, and as he reached his fingers into my hair, tilting my head and deepening the kiss, I also knew it was full of promise.

He was in control, giving me every piece of hope for us as we clung to each other. I could feel myself falling for him. It was fast, but this was Nate. And, for once, I was certain he felt the same about me.

As we continued to kiss on that beach, on our beach, I knew I was in deep. Nothing had ever felt so right. And nothing had ever scared me more.

CHAPTER FIFTEEN

"Do you have sunscreen?" Mom asked.

I waved the bottle above my head with my good hand before stashing it in my bag. Nate had insisted on icing my knuckles last night after their encounter with Johnny's face, so the swelling was down, but they were definitely still a little sore. My mom had been more proud than anything else when we'd told her. She was the one who'd trained me in the art of the right hook.

"Okay great. I have some snacks, and Sarah said she already snagged us a spot with a good view of the comp."

"Great," I said forcefully.

Last night had been magical. But after Nate had dropped me off at my door with one more scorching kiss to my lips and a light one to my bruised knuckles, I'd realized I'd agreed to go to his surfing competition. With our moms. Having kissed a lot the night before.

I was nervous.

"You okay, sweetheart?" Mom asked, coming up beside me and pulling me into a side hug. "I thought you'd be excited to see Nate surf. Did something happen?"

"Yeah, yeah. I'm really excited to see him surf. It's been a long time. I just—" I paused, taking a deep breath. This was my mom. We told each other everything—it's how we survived. "I really like him, Mom. A lot. I'm just nervous."

'Oh, sweetheart, I'm so happy you're finally letting yourself feel it!" She pulled me in for a full hug, holding me there as I burrowed into her. "It's normal to be nervous. That just means it's real. And that is by far the most exciting part."

I nodded as we pulled away, giving her a small smile and convincing myself that she was right. We gathered our bags then headed out the sliding glass door and around the house to the car. The surfing competition was taking place a few towns over, so we had to drive to get there.

After our talk in the kitchen, the drive was filled with laughter and switching between classic rock and classical music. We found parking a few blocks away and made our way down to the beach.

There were pop-up tents everywhere. Some belonged to the schools—offering shelter from the sun for the surfers and storage for their boards—and some belonged to sponsors. Some were local, and some were big brand names. There was a good-sized crowd, but since it was the end of the school season, it was mostly only the hardcore fans and family. There were more than a few girls in bikinis wandering around.

I glanced down at my T-shirt and jean shorts. The T-shirt I'd chosen this morning was special—it was the first one I'd found in the store when picking out clothes for myself, with the Olympic rings on it. It felt right, seeing as Nate had pretty much won our little Olympics the night before.

My jean shorts were different from my normal ones. These had small daisies stitched all over them. I hadn't bothered with a swimsuit—I knew I wouldn't be getting in the water. My long blonde hair fell straight around my face, and I hadn't bothered with makeup this morning. Glancing at the other girls, I wondered if showing up fresh-faced wasn't in style for this type of thing.

"Jess! Ari!" Sarah's voice hauled me out of my thoughts, and I followed Mom across the sand to where Sarah had our three chairs set up. The sky was still overcast since it was early, but the waves looked good.

"Thanks for saving us a spot, Sarah," Mom said as she set her bag down.

"Of course! Nate and I have a tradition of grabbing pumpkin muffins before competitions, and he likes to get here early to get in the headspace. So I always get a pretty good spot."

She beamed, and I could tell how proud she was of her boy. How much she cared about him.

Me too, Sarah. Me too.

"And you girls are right on time! It's almost his heat!"

As Sarah spoke, an announcement came via a man with a megaphone. Sure enough, Nate's name was announced along with three other guys. One of them was Luke.

"They'll line up right in front of us, so we can just hang out here. It's a smaller crowd today, so we don't have to worry as much about people coming to stand in front of us. Thank goodness."

I felt too nervous to sit, but when Sarah and my mom got situated in their chairs, I caved and took the one on the end.

Soon enough, four guys in wetsuits with short boards tucked under their arms ran to the shoreline. The waves lapped their feet as they waited for the signal. One of the others was trying to say something to a surfer with a shaved head, who I recognized as Luke. I chuckled when he ignored the other guy, eyes focused on the incoming swell. I glanced at the other two, looking for those brown curls.

I found them. And those blue eyes were scanning the crowd, searching. When they finally made it to our chairs, Nate gave a small smile to Sarah and my mom before zeroing in on me. His smile grew, making his eyes crinkle with happiness.

Pressing my lips together to keep my smile from being over the top, I gave him a little wave. He gave me a big one back.

The announcer called for the surfers to get ready, and we broke eye contact, our attention drawn towards the loud voice. But before turning to the sea, Nate locked eyes with me one more time. Then he winked.

The horn blared and the surfers ran into the water, jumping onto their boards, and paddling quickly out to the break.

Sarah explained that we probably wouldn't get to talk to Nate until the competition was over. Apparently his coach had a pretty strict rule about no distractions during competitions, as a result of Kyle missing an entire heat to talk to some girls back in their sophomore year.

We got lucky that Nate was in a later heat, because he easily made it to the semi-final round. I mean, I knew he was good, but watching him drop in and make clean cuts like he'd been born for this? It was beautiful. *He* was beautiful.

During the semi-final round, the sun started to melt the overcast away. Nate scored the highest in that round as well, easily outsurfing each of his opponents. Luke had gone out in the semi-final round, taking fourth overall.

Kyle had apparently decided not to surf this comp and was with the coach under their school tent. He and Luke now cheered Nate on as he sat in the water, waiting for one more wave to pad his final score. I watched, entranced as he shook out his wet curls. He looked so peaceful out there, with the water moving and flowing around him and the droplets that clung to his skin glistening in the sun.

"He's really on fire today," Sarah mused, glancing over at me curiously. "I wonder if he has a little extra motivation."

"Well it is his last competition of the school year," I said quickly, tearing my gaze away from Nate and looking at the broken shells I'd been collecting between heats. I'd found some really beautiful ones. *Focus on the shells, Ari.*

"Uh-huh," Sarah said, clearly not convinced. But she was quickly distracted as Nate flipped his board on a dime and started paddling. "Go, baby, go! You've got this, Nate!"

A lot of other voices started cheering as Nate beat out the other surfer. It was clear he was going to win.

He made a few beautiful cuts and rode the wave out until the end, grinning and saluting the crowd before he fell back into the ocean. Sarah and Mom jumped up, cheering loudly and clapping. I rose to my feet as well, setting my shells in my bag. I couldn't help the smile that spread across my face. He was amazing. I wanted to run to him, to hug him tight.

Maybe kiss him again.

"Okay, okay. Wow. That—oh he's just so amazing! So they like to keep things simple at these school comps. They'll present them with their medals right at the shoreline, take some pictures and all that. Then he'll go chat with his coach, and then finally he can come talk to us." Sarah rolled her eyes. "Dumb. But we can still cheer as he gets his picture taken."

As Nate and the other finalists emerged from the water, I drew in a quick breath.

He. Was. Stunning.

He propped up his board and started chatting with one of the other surfers, and I took a second to really take him in. Damp curls, high cheekbones, tanned skin. Those piercing blue eyes.

The presenter announced the placings, and a huge cheer went up for Nate as he was given the first-place medal. He smiled and shook hands with the presenter, then posed for a picture with the other two finalists. Sarah was snapping away from our vantage point with her old-school digital camera as she cheered loudly.

As soon as the pictures were over, his coach was leading him back towards the tent. He barely even had a chance to glance over here—if he'd even wanted to of course.

Sarah and my mom were chatting about the competition and some romance book they'd both been reading as they settled back down in their chairs. I took this as a sign we'd be waiting for Nate for a minute.

Taking in the crowd beginning to disperse, I glanced towards the water. There was no one near it right now. The waves tumbled into the shore, and past the break it looked so peaceful.

I moved away from the chairs, slowly drawn to it.

The rest of the noise faded away as I hesitantly put a foot into the tide. The cold water rushed over my toes, coming up to my ankle, and I quickly put the other foot in as well, loving the shock to my system.

The ocean had always been my place. Summers were my escape. And the water was where I'd spent most of my time. I still couldn't tell if it was nostalgia or real feelings, but a calm settled over me. There was fear too. I wasn't ready to surf. Or even to go for a swim. But this small step was big for me. And I loved it.

"Nathan!" I heard a female voice yell.

It wasn't Sarah's. In fact, when I turned, I saw Nate standing by our moms with an arm looped around his mom's shoulders and his medal hanging from her neck. A group of bikini-clad girls were making their way towards him. I was shocked by the openly hungry look in their eyes.

Jeez, girls, his mom is literally right there.

And so was I. But they didn't know what we were. I mean, neither did I, but the jealousy and insecurity still rampaged through me.

Nate's expression morphed into something akin to fear. Sarah nudged him, nodding towards where I stood. Relief washed over his face, and he whispered something to his mom before heading my direction.

"Nathan!" the girls called again.

"Sorry, ladies." He broke into a jog. He was a few steps from me. "I have someone special I have to talk to."

I barely had time to register that one of the girls scoffed. Actually scoffed. They all looked disgruntled as they stomped away.

But there was no time to process their reaction because in a split-second, Nate reached me, scooping me into his arms and spinning me around. I wrapped my arms tight around his neck, laughing as we spun. Water and sand flew out around us, but I didn't care.

When we finally stopped spinning, he didn't set me down. He had me by the legs, so I was a good head above him. I rested my hands on his shoulders to steady myself as I looked down at him. He'd pulled his wetsuit off his upper body, leaving his chest and arms bare.

"Hey, pretty girl," he said softly.

"Hey, champ," I replied breathlessly.

He slowly loosened his grip, letting me basically slide down the front of his body until my toes hit the water. Once I was back on my feet, I glanced over to where our mothers were. Thankfully, the chairs were gone, and I saw just my bag left—their figures were retreating towards the parking lot.

"I asked the moms if I could take you out to a victory lunch." He smiled as I turned my head back to him. "You know, to celebrate."

I laughed. "Shouldn't I be taking you to a victory lunch?" I asked, letting my hands wander into the wet curls at the nape of his neck. I couldn't help it—they'd been calling to me all day.

He smiled, leaning closer so his forehead rested on mine.

"I mean, technically yes." He glanced down at my shirt. "Especially since I'm a double winner."

"I knew you'd get it." I pulled my head back as I laughed. "See?"

"Yes, yes. But I have a place I want to show you."

"Oh yeah?"

"Yeah. Plus, they have a really good special sauce." He grinned.

I opened my mouth to reply, but another male voice I was coming to know well interrupted us.

"Nate!" Luke walked over, Kyle jogging behind him to keep up. "Sorry to interrupt, man, but we're heading out. Congrats on the win."

When they reached us, I quickly dropped my arms from around Nate. He rolled his eyes at me before grabbing my hand.

"Yeah, congrats on everything." Kyle laughed, glancing at us with knowing eyes.

A blush quickly worked its way up my neck, but Nate just grinned. "Thanks, guys."

"You heading to lunch?" Kyle asked.

Nate nodded. "Yep. Gotta show her Pedro's. You boys wanna join?"

"Court's still at work and she's already bummed about missing the comp, so I'm probably gonna go visit her then head home. But if you're still there, it's so close I might drop by." Luke shrugged noncommittally. "I'll text you."

"Yeah, he's got girl stuff and I've got mandatory 'we're still a family' Saturdays." Kyle made a gagging noise. "I'd love to come, but you two have fun. But not too much fun—you know what I'm sayin'?"

He winked obnoxiously, and both Nate and Luke rolled their eyes.

"Tell Court I say hi," Nate said as he and Luke did that weird bro hug thing. He kept my hand in his as he did it with Kyle too, then the guys headed towards the parking lot.

When he turned back to me, I gave him a timid smile as he pushed my hair behind my ear.

"Who's Court?" I asked.

"Oh, that's Luke's girl. She's cool. She's normally here to support, but she couldn't get her shift switched around this time." He smiled as he pulled me a little closer. My breath quickened as he leaned closer. "I guess it's just us."

"I guess so," I barely whispered before he put his lips on mine. That electricity shot through me again as I dropped his hand to wrap my arms around his neck, pushing to my tiptoes as I kissed him back. His hands went to my waist as he pulled away slowly. Then he pressed another quick kiss to my lips. Then another. Then one more. Then he finally mumbled some coherent words against my lips.

"How do you feel about tacos?"

CHAPTER SIXTEEN

Walking into Pedro's Taco Shop was one of the new highlights of my life. First of all, Nate had changed and was wearing a gray T-shirt that stretched across his chest really nicely. And he was holding my non-bruised hand as the sweet, sweet smell of flour tortillas and taco meat hit me.

Paradise.

"Hey, Nate! How'd it go?" the man behind the grill called.

"Pretty good, Pedro! The surf was really good, so it made for some fun competition," he called back.

Okay. They were on a first-name basis.

"Hey, boy, who's the pretty girl?"

"Someone special," Nate answered as he smiled down at me, tugging me towards a booth in the corner.

As he slipped into one side, I scooted into the other, setting my bag on the seat before I glanced around. This was definitely a hole-in-the-wall-type place. There were only a few other people seated around, but they all looked overjoyed to be there, though the booths were old and tattered, and the decor was pretty tacky. Some mariachi music played from an old radio set up on the bar.

"Hey, *hermano*, Pedro's cooking up two orders of your regular if that's cool." A young guy, probably early twenties if I had to guess, slid a soda in front of Nate before resting an arm on the top of the booth. "What can I get for you to drink, miss?"

"Um, do you have lemonade?"

"Yes, miss. I'll have that right out."

"Thanks." I gave him a small smile.

"Thanks, T," Nate said, giving him a nod.

The guy, T apparently, nodded back and brought my lemonade over quickly.

"So, you on a first-name basis with every restaurant owner in Avila Beach?" I asked as I took a sip.

Nate just chuckled, swirling his straw in his Coke. "Nope, just with Pedro. He moved here from Mexico about… thirty years ago now. He's a legend around here." He leaned forward, like he was sharing a secret. "When you try his sweet chicken tacos, you'll understand."

"Sweet chicken?" I asked skeptically, but that just made him nod almost reverently.

"Ari, I swear to you. This will make even your mom's enchiladas become your second-favorite Mexican food." As soon as he finished speaking, he held both hands up as I gasped dramatically. "I know, I know."

"That's some blasphemy right there, Nathaniel Rentz."

"Oh, we pulled out the full name."

"You know my mom's enchiladas are my all-time favorite food."

"I am aware."

"Bold."

"The bold do get the biggest prizes." He smirked, snaking his hand across the table so he could grab mine and lace our fingers together. "At least, that's what I'm hoping."

Speechless, I just ducked my head.

T saved me at that moment, sliding a basket with three steaming tacos in front of each of us and giving me an excuse to pull my hand back from Nate's electric touch.

As Nate and T exchanged a few more words, I took in my food. The tacos smelled delicious, but what caught my surprise were the three small dishes in my basket. I glanced at Nate's—he had the same.

Sour cream, salsa, and guacamole on the side—what I always had when I ate Mexican food. I smiled to myself.

"The special sauce is really what you gotta try," Nate explained as he pointed to another small dish that T had placed on the table between us.

We were alone again, and I could feel the excitement radiating off Nate.

"Here, can I see your tacos? Do you trust me?"

I met his eyes. The way he said it implied much more than just trusting him with my tacos, although that was a huge form of trust as it was. Something shifted between us as I pushed my taco basket towards him.

"Yeah, I trust you."

Oh, that smile.

Nate got to work adding different combinations of our condiment selection to my tacos. When he finally finished, he slowly pushed my basket back to me.

"Okay. Get ready to be the happiest you've ever been."

I hesitantly picked up what looked like vomit in a tortilla. It still smelled good. That was enough for my starving stomach.

As soon as I took a bite, I raised my eyes to Nate's expectant face. "Oh no. My mom is gonna be so pissed."

"Rest in peace, Jess's enchiladas."

CHAPTER SEVENTEEN

The next weeks were full of Nathan. We spent every waking second we could together, just being happy for no reason at all. I spent all day holding Nate's hand as we walked the beach, went to the pier, and ate at every hole-in-the-wall restaurant in town. We preferred Pedro's obviously, but part of our deal was trying different things. Which we reluctantly did.

I "helped" him while he fixed the roof, the car, or whatever else Sarah needed done. Meaning I talked to him and handed him tools he needed. He didn't try to ask me about what happened, but I knew it was something that bugged him. Sometimes I'd freeze up around a big crowd; other times I would hesitate to speak or completely zone out. The first few times, he would try to overcompensate by getting up in my face and trying to snap me out of it. When he realized that only made things worse, he completely changed tactics. Now, when I froze up or zoned out, he'd take my hand and pull me aside so I could breathe for a second.

Nate was so patient. On the surface at least.

I could tell it was killing him to not ask, and I knew we'd have to have the conversation someday. But I was enjoying being a teenage girl spending the summer with a boy she really liked. I spent every night in his arms as we watched the sunset and talked for hours, until he dropped me off at my room before our moms got too suspicious. Of course, there were plenty of stolen kisses and pretending that Mom and Sarah still believed we were just friends.

It was heaven.

One morning, I rolled out of bed and stumbled downstairs in a haze. My nightmares had been really bad—Mom had to come in a few times and wake me up, I was screaming so loud. Thankfully, Nate was a heavy sleeper.

The nightmares had started a week or so after we'd arrived at Avila Beach. They were always the same, that terrifying night playing on a loop. Nate never said anything, and I knew he would have if he'd heard them.

I yawned, rubbing the tiredness out of my eyes as I spotted a note on the counter.

Sweetheart,

Nate is dropping us old women off at the farmers' market. Didn't want to walk in the morning fog but did want to walk in the glorious sunshine later. Love you, have a great day!

—The moms

I smiled. If anyone deserved to go off and have some fun, it was our moms. Mom had been more relaxed in the last month than I'd seen her in years. Being with Nate, peace had settled around me too. It was intoxicating, and I always needed more of it. More of him.

Not feeling super hungry, I went upstairs to change into my swimsuit. While I knew I wasn't going to go into the ocean today, I also knew I needed to take baby steps. Start letting go, like Mom had said.

So I grabbed that beautiful black-and-white one-piece and started looking for a sundress to wear over the top. I glanced down at the swimsuit, noticing that the open back actually had a beautiful crisscross pattern. Huh. Maybe there was more to the plain, simple things than you could initially see.

Choosing a sundress wasn't a regular occurrence for me. I'd been wearing my stunning wardrobe of oversized graphic tees and jean shorts almost religiously, but it wouldn't hurt to change it up a bit.

My gaze landed on a dress shoved in the corner of the closet. Pushed back behind bright yellows and neon pinks, this sundress was blue—not a bright blue that one would expect to find in Sarah's closet but a deep blue. Like the ocean. My breath caught as I pulled out the hanger to get a better look at it. There was something about the color; it made my heart beat faster. It was something other than the water. What did it remind me of?

Deciding it would come to me, I tugged off my pajamas and tossed them in the hamper, trying to steady my breathing as I slipped on my swimsuit. Why was even this hard for me? But I knew why. Glimpses of my nightmares came rushing back to me. Shaking them away, I reached for that blue fabric.

It was soft. It felt peaceful. As I slipped it over my head, a soft smile eased the tension that etched my face. I glanced at myself in the full-length mirror. It was beautiful, with thick straps that covered my shoulders and a full skirt that ended mid-thigh; it made me feel every inch the princess I'd told Nate I wasn't.

I'd just finished pulling a brush through my matted hair when I heard a noise at the door. Quickly turning, I saw him leaning against the doorframe. Nate. The way he was looking at me, the careful way his gaze traveled over my body, made my pulse pick up and my chest tighten in anticipation.

"Ari." His voice was low, gruff.

I blinked at him, trying to figure out why he was looking at me like that. "Nate, what's wrong?"

He just shook his head, staring at me and not saying a word.

"Nate, you're freaking me out. Is something wrong? Are the moms okay?" Fear raced through me. Had something happened to my mom? Was *he* here?

"No, no. The moms are okay." He took a step into the room. "Ari, do you even know how beautiful you are?"

Oh. *Oh.* A blush worked its way across my entire body. I realized that the look in his eyes was something warm, something intimate. Butterflies were swarming in my stomach. Not just flying, swarming.

"Um, Nate, I just rolled out of bed. I'm definitely not—"

Before I could finish my sentence, Nate closed the distance between us, crashing his lips down on mine. We'd kissed a lot over the weeks, but it had always been slow and sweet.

After that first night, Nate had let me take the lead on how far things went. Always pulled away before things could get too heated. But this kiss was filled with so much emotion. It felt desperate, but the best kind of desperate.

Nate weaved his hands through my hair, holding my face in place as the kiss deepened and changed. My hands moved their way across Nate's chest, playing with his jaw and teasing the ends of his hair in the way I'd recently learned he really liked.

Smiling against my lips, Nate pulled me even closer to his body. I was tall, but Nate was really tall. And I loved going up on my tiptoes to return his kiss.

Looping my arms around his neck, I fought to get some sort of leverage, but Nate wasn't having it. His hands were deep in my hair, moving my head this way and that. I gasped, surprised by this new forwardness.

Nate pulled back, just enough to see my face. "Is this okay?" Hesitancy flashed in his eyes as he asked.

I was a complete mess. His kiss had left me speechless. I was fumbling for coherent thoughts, let alone words.

"I—um, uh. Yes. Yes, it's definitely okay. More than okay. I just—" I took a deep breath. "I guess I'm just wondering where all that came from?"

"Yeah, sorry about that. Ari, you're just so stunning I couldn't help it. And when I saw you looking in the mirror, you were missing that sad look and—"

"Sad look?" I asked.

Moving one hand from where it was still tangled in my hair, he cupped my cheek and looked deep into my eyes. I suddenly realized what the sundress color had reminded me of—it was the exact shade of the eyes that were now staring deep into my soul, as if they could read my every thought. Nate's eyes.

"Even when you were little, when something was bothering you, you would get this look. Like you were just waiting for everything to come crashing down." He smiled softly. "You haven't lost that look since you've been back. It's always there—even when you're laughing or smiling, it's in your eyes. Like you're waiting for something to go wrong."

Tears I didn't want to acknowledge were threatening to overflow. My gaze dropped, and I hoped he wouldn't see how much I wanted to give my sadness away. How much I wanted to tell him everything. How much I wanted to just *be*.

"Ari," he whispered, moving my head back up and forcing my eyes to meet his. "For that one moment, that sadness was gone. You looked like an eighteen-year-old girl, realizing that she looks stunning in a sundress. Baby, why do you always have that sadness? What's going on? What am I missing?"

A single tear rolled down my face. Then another. I knew he would bring it up again. Knew he was only trying to help.

He moved the hand that had still been locked in my hair to my other cheek, so he was cradling my face, his thumbs gently swiping at my tears. The way he was looking at me, like he was ready to take on the world for me, was almost enough to break me.

Almost.

"Nate. I—I just—" I took a deep breath, trying to hold back any more tears. I opened my mouth to tell him something, anything. I wanted so badly to share a piece of what was happening with him. But the words were stuck in my throat. If only he knew who I really was, he would never look at me the same. He would never want to put his lips on mine again. Never hold my hand.

"Baby, please," he whispered again, this time urgently.

It hadn't escaped my notice that he'd called me "baby" twice now. This was new. But even with the war going on in my head, my heart leaped at the endearment. I couldn't help it.

"Please let me help. I want to help. I want to fix it, but I can't if I don't know what's broken."

Broken.

Broken.

He wanted to fix it, because that's who he was. He was a fixer. This was all this was. I was something broken, and he wanted to fix it. When his dad left, he'd taken care of his mom. When I'd broken my surfboard when I was twelve, he'd helped me earn enough to buy a new one. When my mom had been missing my dad, he'd baked her favorite cookies and quietly placed them in front of her. Even in the short time we'd been together, he was always helping fix something. If there was a problem, Nate fixed it—and I had a problem.

Of course he wanted to fix me, but I couldn't let him try. He wouldn't be able to. This beautiful boy with the most loving heart would only get sucked into my sadness. It would break him, and I couldn't let that happen.

Using all the strength I could muster, I put my hands on Nate's chest and pushed him away. Stumbling back in surprise, Nate looked at me with wide eyes.

"That's the problem, Nate. This can't be fixed. None of this can be fixed." Taking a gulp of air, I looked into those deep-blue eyes. It took everything in me not to look away. "I just—I—I can't. I can't. It's too much, and if you knew, if you knew, you wouldn't want to ever look at me again. I'm broken. I'm so unbelievably broken, and you don't deserve any of this. You don't deserve to be kept in the dark. You don't deserve to be hurt by the truth. You don't deserve to be stuck with me. There is no win here, Nate."

"Ari. Ari, hey, there's nothing you could say that would—" His eyes were wide as he reached for me.

I forced myself not to reach back and took another step away. "There is, Nate—there's so much lost time between the girl you knew and the girl I am now."

I'd reached full hysteria, words and sobs tumbling out of my mouth and tears streaming down my face. He needed to understand. To know that he was too good for me. He was far too good for me.

"You—You'll realize that soon enough. It doesn't matter what you felt for me when we were kids, because that girl doesn't exist anymore. We're both so different now, and so different from each other. And—and it hurts because I am falling so hard for you, for this you. For the boy who holds my hand and gets lost staring at the sea and who makes me feel everything. But it's not fair to you that I'm not the same. I'm not whole, Nate. I'm broken. I'm broken, and I can't—I can't—"

When did breathing get so hard? My lungs felt tight, like the air was closing in around them. I tried to take a deep breath, but it was shallow. Not enough. Not nearly enough. Blackness crept into the edges of my vision, and I felt my body sway—but a strong arm looped around my waist, the other coming to hold my head up.

"Whoa, whoa. Ari, breathe. Here, hold on. Sit down." He led me to the bed, and we sat down together.

Without a word, he shuffled back to where the bed met the wall, leaning against it and softly pulling me with him. One gentle tug, and I was nestled against his chest, his strong arms wrapped around me.

Still gasping for breath, with our legs tangled together and Nate's hand rubbing small circles on my back, I tried to focus on his voice.

"Listen to my voice, baby. Breathe in deep, and hold it. Okay, now breathe out. Good. Good. Now again. You can do it, Ari. In. Hold. Now out again. Good."

He repeated that four or five more times until my breathing was finally even, and my body had stopped shaking. He was still holding me close, rubbing circles on my back as though he had all the time in the world to sit there and hold me.

Finally, peaceful but more than a little embarrassed, I leaned back hesitantly to look up at him.

I trembled as I saw the pain in his face. The sadness. The vulnerability in those beautiful blue eyes. Still hesitant, not knowing what his reaction to my complete breakdown would be, I moved to give him some space.

"No, Ari." His arms tightened around me. "You don't get to run away this time. We're going to talk about this. Work through this. Because you are worth it to me, okay?"

A small spark of joy ran through me at his words. This boy.

"Okay." I gave him a small smile, and he returned it. "Nate, how did you know what to do? When I started to, um, black out, how did you know how to bring me back?"

Now it was Nate's turn to look uncomfortable. He dropped his gaze, glancing over at my windowsill. At my seashells. A small smile formed on his lips, almost taking away the pain there. Almost.

Working up my courage, I put my hand on his cheek, turning his head back to meet my eyes.

He sighed and leaned into my hand. "Ari, you're not the only one who has panic attacks."

He gave me a soft smile, but I finally understood what he'd meant about my eyes. The sadness he'd spoken of lived in his at that moment, despite his relaxed posture and smile.

"After my dad left, I started getting these nightmares. Nightmares that my mom would leave too. That I would wake up one day and there would be nobody left. I'd be alone."

My heart broke at the thought, at little Nate with his tender heart, scared of being abandoned. Scared of being left behind. I pressed my lips together as he continued.

"I would wake up screaming. The first time, my mom ran into my room just as freaked out and terrified as I was. But after that, she would just walk in, pick me up, and rock me until I settled like nothing was wrong with me. She would coach my breathing."

He took a breath, pushing my hair behind my ear. "It used to be every night, but slowly the nightmares only started coming every few days, once a week, once a month, until it was only every once in a while and without the screams. Usually when something happens during the day to trigger them."

He paused and suddenly looked a little ashamed.

I tilted my head, puzzled at this new emotion written so freely on his face. "What triggers it?" I asked softly.

"Normally when I start to get attached to something or someone. Me and Ma call it 'octopus suction theory.'" He chuckled. "I thought it was cooler when I was fifteen than saying I get a rush of subconscious fear whenever anyone gets close enough to me that I could care about them. Close enough that it could hurt when they leave."

I smiled softly, but something about his sentence bugged me.

"Wait, you said when." It was a statement.

"Yeah." Another statement.

"You think everyone is going to leave you?"

The look in his eyes was all the answer I needed. Oh.

"When was the last time you had a nightmare?"

He gave me a small smile, running his hand through my hair and twirling the ends around his fingers.

"Nate?"

"You know how you said I cared about the girl you were but not about the girl you are now?"

Grimacing at my harsh words, I gave a small nod.

"Ari, I didn't have a nightmare for a year until the night we kissed on the beach. Until after we went to the caves, after you'd passed out and scared me half to death, after you punched Johnny in the face. Until after we spent time to-gether, talking and laughing and just being together. Not as kids. As us—Nathaniel Rentz, a nineteen-year-old boy with amazing muscles and stunning good looks."

I gave him a small giggle.

He smiled, but then his eyes grew serious as he took my face in both his hands, forcing me to look directly at him. "And Arielle Hansen, eighteen-year-old girl. A little bit sad, but oh so beautiful. Kind enough to always think of everyone else first. Stubborn enough to walk away when an idiot keeps pushing her to open up and she needs more time. Selfless enough to come back to that idiot and give him another chance. Collector of broken seashells. Always the most beautiful broken ones. A girl who has a tendency to run but not because she doesn't care. Because she cares too much. This girl. The one right here in front of me. This is the girl I'm falling for. Yes, I was half in love with you when we were kids. Yes, I held on to that girl because she was my best friend and everything good in my world. But one look into your beautiful, sad eyes and feelings I never had when we were kids came. Because of who you are now."

He took a breath. I was stunned. Near speechless.

"Oh."

"Yeah, oh." He pulled my face closer.

I gasped. We were so close now I could feel his lips against mine as he spoke. My eyes shut on their own, waiting.

After a pause, he whispered, "Ari, no one has ever made me feel the way you do. And I know this is new and fast, and I know something's wrong. I'm so sorry for pushing you. For getting all up in your face about it. I just, I feel so—"

"Helpless?" I asked.

I felt him nod.

"I want to protect you, Ari." He took another deep breath. "I don't know if I can watch you leave again and not know if you're coming back."

He knew my heart so well. He knew me. Knew I wanted to run. Knew I was broken. And yet, instead of letting me go before we got too deep, he was fighting.

I leaned forward and pressed a gentle kiss to his lips. He kissed me back softly, almost hesitantly. Like he didn't want to scare me.

I pulled back, resting my forehead against his. "I know. I'm sorry I freaked out. I just—" I took another deep breath. Apparently hard conversations required a lot of those. "I'm just a girl who always runs away, trying to stay. Because the boy who's asking me to stay is a boy who wants to protect me from things that have already happened. And I don't know how fair that is. But I'm trying. I'm trying to be a girl who stays, Nate."

"Ari, I don't want you to be a girl who stays. I want you to be a girl who feels like she can."

There were no words, no answer I could give that would ever make sense. It would never fit the way Nate had just unknowingly filled a hole in my heart. How he so perfectly knew how I felt. So I didn't say anything. Instead, I looked into the eyes of my beautiful boy and pushed my lips to his again.

There was no hesitancy this time.

He pulled me even closer, his hands still cradling my head, and the kiss grew deeper, his lips moving against mine with so much confidence. With so much feeling. It was like we'd broken through a wall, and Nate was finally letting himself take the lead—and I was finally letting him.

His hands worked their way through my hair, and it took everything in me not to gasp. I should have felt nervous. Nate had no idea he was the only boy I'd ever kissed. Maybe he'd guessed, but I'd never told him. And even then, he'd never kissed me like this before. That first night had only been a taste of how much passion Nathaniel Rentz could put into a kiss. And I loved it.

As if he could hear my thoughts, he moved against me, lightly guiding me until I was lying back on the bed and he was above me. His lips never left mine. He was careful to keep his weight off me, moving his hands so he rested his elbows on either side of my head.

My hands took over. They were on his chest, then in his hair. Then they were cupping his face, tracing his jawline as we kissed and kissed and kissed.

When we finally broke apart, I was breathless. But Nate wasn't done yet. He looked at me, and I knew—my heart was his. Fully. Undeniably. And it had decided on a strict no-return policy.

As he gently placed a kiss on my forehead, then my cheek, then a featherlight one on my neck, I knew. I didn't feel like I could stay just yet, but I wanted to.

And that was more than I'd ever been able to give him.

With one more achingly soft kiss on my lips, Nate dropped down beside me, lying on his side and turning my body to face him before resting his hand on my hip.

"Ari?"

"Hm?"

"Are we tapped out on emotional things for the day, or can I show you something real quick?" he asked, all calm and confident, as if we hadn't just kissed like that. But one look at his flushed cheeks and I knew he was feeling just as much as I was.

"That depends. Are we doing anything else emotionally taxing today?" I smiled at him as he laughed, pushing my hair away from my face and twirling a few strands in his fingers. My voice shook a little, but that kiss had given me a determination to just be us. To let the sadness fade for a bit.

"No, I was actually coming up here to ask if you wanted to go to the arcade before, ya know—"

"Emotional breakdown and post-emotional breakdown makeout?"

He laughed at me again. My voice had held a bit stronger this time.

"Woman, as glad as I am that you've gotten your sass back so fast, can you let me finish?"

He could barely speak without laughing, and I loved the sound so much I decided one more joke wouldn't hurt.

"Oh, so now I'm 'baby' and 'woman'? Those seem like opposites if you ask me," I said, tilting my head as I challenged him, my voice now completely even. "Yeah, even mid-breakdown I pay attention. You called me 'baby' several times. That's new."

"Is that okay with you? I mean, after what we just did, I think I'm allowed to call you something other than just Ari," he responded smartly, meeting my challenge like he always did.

I pretended to think for a moment, really playing into mulling it over. "Fine, I guess I can learn to love it."

"Great! Alright, one more stop and then the arcade!" He smacked a chaste kiss to my lips then hopped over me, making the bed bounce as he did. I cried out in protest, but he just grabbed my hand and dragged me to my feet. "Come on, babe—let's hustle! I've been saving my nickels just to show off my gaming skills and beat all those crap ten-year-olds for weeks!"

I giggled, knowing he had not in fact been saving his nickels but that he did fully intend to destroy some ten-year-olds. He was really just a big kid at heart.

He pulled me by the hand, leading us out of my room and down the hall to his.

"Um, Nate, I hate to break it to you, but I've definitely already seen your room before." I laughed as he excitedly opened the door.

"Haha, very funny. Get in here," he deadpanned as he yanked me through the doorway.

Quickly letting my hand drop, he hurried over to his closet. I took the second alone to look at his room. Yes, I'd been here before but not since I'd been back. I wasn't sure why we never seemed to hang out in his room. It was always the beach, or downstairs, sometimes my room. But never his.

His walls were still crisp white. Nate could never decide what color was his favorite when he was little, so he'd just left it white. His favorite color didn't become green until later. But the walls were covered with posters and handwritten notes and pictures. Most of the pictures were older, ones of him and his mom from when he was little. Some were newer.

I recognized Kyle and Luke—the three boys grinning, holding surfboards and medals. There were quite a few pictures like that. Some Nate had definitely taken himself. That boy was so talented. I'd seen him in action with his camera a few times since I'd arrived, and it was clear he loved it. The emotion that came through his pictures was stunning.

But the ones that took me by surprise were the ones of us. Nate with his arm slung around me when we were just little kids, all scrawny arms and freckled noses. A few years later, when I won my first surfing competition. A wide smile dominated my face, surfboard and medal in hand, while Nate once again had his arm around my shoulders. But in this photo, he wasn't looking at the camera. He was looking at me.

Many more pictures of us covered the wall—small moments captured from the childhood summers we'd shared. Some pictures we were both beaming at the camera; in others Nate was looking happily at me. In others, I was looking longingly at him.

But it was the two picture frames on his nightstand that took my breath away.

In one frame, there was a picture of the four of us sitting on the porch steps. Sarah held a very young me on her lap, cuddling me close and squishing our faces together as we laughed. Next to us, my mom was smiling wide as Nate stood behind her, looping his arms around her neck and giving a toothy grin. This was the only family I'd ever known. And we'd always been happier together than we'd ever been apart.

The other picture frame was obviously newer, just a simple black frame, but I recognized the picture it held. It was from a week ago, when we'd gone out with Luke and Kyle to Pedro's. Kyle had obviously taken the picture, since he and

Luke had sat across from us in the booth and Luke never took a picture of his own free will. As in every other image, Nate's arm was slung around my shoulders, but now he was pulling me closer than before. We were turned towards each other, my eyes closed as I laughed, my hair whipping around my face, and I was surprised by how carefree I looked. How insanely happy and relaxed.

But what truly stunned me was Nate's face.

He was looking down at me, his signature half-smile making the world go round. His eyes were locked on me, and he was looking at me like I was something precious. Like he would do anything to be near me.

I was so entranced by the photo that I didn't hear Nate close the closet door and come up behind me. A small gasp of surprise escaped me as Nate looped an arm around my waist, pulling me back against him.

"I think that might be one of my new favorite pictures," he whispered, his breath tickling my ear and causing a shiver to go down my spine.

I gulped, not fully trusting myself to speak right away.

"Mine too," I finally whispered back, my voice tight.

Nate pressed a light kiss to my neck, and my heart beat even faster. Too overwhelmed with everything, I leaned back into him and closed my eyes as he tucked his head onto my shoulder.

We stood like that, just being there for a moment, until Nate's voice whispered to me again.

"Hey, Ari, are you ready for your surprise?"

I nodded, opening my eyes and turning towards him. He kept his hand on my waist as I faced him, ensuring I stayed close. Out the corner of my eye, I noticed his other hand was in a fist at his side. My eyes followed it as he raised the fist level with my face then opened it.

Dangling from his fingers was a necklace. But not just any necklace—this was a simple string, and on the end was a seashell.

I reached out, grasping the shell between my fingers. My breath halted as I ran my fingers over the rough edges.

"A broken shell," I whispered breathlessly. Finally looking into Nate's eyes, I was struck by the feeling I saw there.

"That last summer you were here, we spent almost every morning looking for broken seashells. You were so particular about what ones you would keep. That night before you left, the night you kissed me…" He paused for a second, taking a deep breath. "That night you kissed me I had this in my pocket. I'd found it a few days before, and Mom had helped me drill a hole and put it on this crappy string. I remember thinking that you'd love it. That it was just the type of shell you'd been searching for."

"It is. Perfect size, perfect color, beautifully—"

"Broken. That was always what we hunted for on those mornings. It was your strictest requirement. But after you kissed me and ran, I was determined to give it to you. To tell you how much I liked you. I thought you'd love it so much, you'd come back the next summer and we'd be together."

Still dangling the necklace, he gave a sad chuckle. "But now, I just want you to have it. Because every time I look at it, it reminds me of you. How perfect you are. Even though you see yourself as broken, you're what I've been searching for. As cliche as that is, it's true. You're all I've ever been looking for, even when I didn't know it."

I couldn't breathe. Not at all. His words had stolen the air right from my lungs. Was this what happiness felt like? I could almost burst from the feeling.

Slowly, as if trying not to scare me, Nate dropped his hands from my waist, walked behind me, and placed the string around my neck, the shell sitting perfectly an inch above my neckline.

As he finished tying it into place, I reached up, touching it again. "Nate," I whispered.

He came in front of me once more but kept his hands to himself. He scratched the back of his head as I pushed my hair behind my ear. His eyes told me everything I needed to know. He was nervous.

"If you don't like it, you don't have to wear it. I just thought, you know, I never got to give it to you when we were kids and it's always been yours, so I just—I mean—"

He stopped talking as I went on my tiptoes and pressed my lips to his. I kept my body separate from his, so only our lips were touching.

Leaning back just enough to look into his eyes, I reached up and brushed his shaggy hair out of his eyes. "I love it," I whispered, dropping my hand back by my side. Another sentence with love in it was on the tip of my tongue, but I bit my bottom lip to keep it from spilling out.

Apparently, that was too much for Nate, because he put his hands on either side of my face and looked at me seriously. "Ari, if we're ever going to make it to the arcade today, you've got to stop making me want to make out with you."

I was so stunned I couldn't even respond as he dropped another quick kiss to my lips and grabbed my hand.

"Okay, gorgeous, let's get going. We have ten-year-olds to beat."

I couldn't hold back my giggles as he dragged me through the house to the back door, only pausing so we could slip on our shoes and leave a note for the moms.

As I fell asleep that night, I touched my broken-shell necklace. I'd voiced parts of my darkest fears to Nate, and he hadn't run away. That shattered everything I'd learned to believe about myself.

Lying in my bed, for the first time in a long time, there was no part of me stressing about the future. No part of me was replaying every second before we'd driven back into Avila Beach. The only thing I could think about was Nate. How he'd pushed my hair back and held me as he'd helped me breathe. How he'd held on to the necklace with the hope that one day I would come back. Was this what peace felt like? Like you couldn't even see past tomorrow because all that mattered was the beauty of the now? If that was what peace felt like, then I loved it, and more than that, I loved a boy. I wanted him for always. And nothing else mattered.

CHAPTER EIGHTEEN

A week later, Nate decided to try and convince me that I should come surf with him again. We were lying on the beach, his head in my lap, as another beautiful day was fading into starlight. The light-pink hues of the sunset softened the blue of the sky, mixing with the wispy clouds and filling my heart with a contented kind of peace.

"Come on, Ari," he whined, sounding like a pouty little kid. "Just once? You've been here for weeks now."

"I don't know," I said softly, my voice almost breaking. I was still uncertain.

The ocean was too deep, too blue, too peaceful. I was too dirty, too damaged, too scared. I had moments where I felt peace, but I wasn't *at* peace. I had finally, somewhat, admitted to myself why I couldn't surf. I was scared. But I was also scared Nate wouldn't understand. Since my complete meltdown, Nate hadn't brought *it* up again. We avoided all mention of the past. We focused on the now. We were sickeningly happy. It filled me with guilt.

Mom and I had been spending some more time together too. We would read books together in the afternoon before she took her nap, and she'd even taken me to the farmers' market. While the crowd had given me anxiety at first, seeing her so at ease had instantly loosened me up, though I knew she still worried about me as much as I worried about her.

I thought back to her words.

"Ari, I love how much you've opened up with Nate, but don't you think you need some girlfriends? You know, like a normal teenager?" she'd asked hopefully. We'd been looking at some hand-stitched handbags at a particularly eccentric woman's stall. Thankfully she'd been with another customer, telling them all about how her third husband had ended up being a mafia boss. Or maybe it was a Russian emperor. It was apparently subject to change.

"Mom. Several things. One"—I'd started counting out my fingers—"since when have I been a normal teenager? Two, most of the girls around here want to run me over with their car so Nate will stop spending time with me and give them the time of day. And three…"

I'd paused. I was trying. I was. But there was only so much a girl could do.

"Three?" Mom had pushed.

"Three, I think letting Nate in as much as I have is scary enough. There are days even he has to push me to open up. It's just—I don't—" I'd taken a deep breath, trying to center myself.

Setting down the rather interesting handbag I'd been looking at, I'd turned so I was fully facing my mom. "I'm trying, Mom. I am. I'm trying to live. But even before, it was hard for me to just up and make friends. Now it feels impossible. The only thing that feels right is Nate. His friends are nice, and sometimes we hang out with them, but he knows me. I think because he knows who I used to be, it gives me hope that I can become more than this shell of myself. Maybe if I meet someone and it just clicks, but I just can't even think about trying to really get to know someone completely new. It's too much, Mom."

As soon as I'd finished, she'd wrapped her arms around me and pulled me tight, cradling the back of my head with one hand.

"Oh, my sweet Ari. I know you're trying. And you've given so much of yourself to Nate, and I love that you have. You've never really had a normal shot at making your own friends is all." She'd pulled back, tears in her eyes as she ran a hand through my hair. "I just worry about you."

"Thanks, Mom. I worry about you too. I worry about what's going to happen to us," I'd whispered. Our savings were low. We couldn't live at the beach house forever, and we were too stubborn to live off the Rentzes any longer than we had to.

Mom had nodded, tilting her head to the side before she spoke again. "I know, sweetheart. Maybe, just this once, we can enjoy ourselves before we have to survive again. We can start to live again."

A tear had escaped her eye and rolled down her cheek. I'd felt it too—this peace and hope was so overwhelming.

"Mom, I want that too. More than anything. But we can't let him find us. We can't." I'd started to shake my head quickly, the panic starting to come quickly. I'd taken another deep breath, focusing on the sounds around me. In and out. In and out.

Mom had pulled me into a hug again. "We're doing all we can, Arielle. We're lying low, not putting our names anywhere legal, not even trying to create fake identities because the risk is too great. He'll either give up or find us, and only time will tell. But we'll handle whatever comes our way—that's all I can promise you, baby."

I'd nodded into Mom's shoulder, holding her tight in the middle of that farmers' market, until we'd pulled apart and smiled at each other. A promise to be happy while we could.

I was brought back to the present when Nate flicked my arm once. Twice. The third time, I grabbed his hand, which of course he turned into a move and laced his fingers with mine.

"What?" I grumbled, faking annoyance. I couldn't be truly annoyed, because he was way too cute.

"But what if a hot surfer helped you learn?" He tilted his head back, straining to see my face.

It was like he'd heard my thoughts. His face was lit up with joy, giddy and expectant, and I laughed, delighted at his humor. I could always depend on that. He was the sunshine to my storm clouds.

"Well I'm not sure Kyle would be up for that." I leaned my face close to his as I teased him.

It only took him a second to lurch from his comfortable sprawl, release my hand, and turn to face me. He gave me a shocked look, complete with a sound effect.

"Plus, if I remember correctly, I always won the surfing competitions we entered."

"Okay, that's it."

As he sprang to his feet, I recognized the mischievous glint in his eye. I began to get up, moving backwards as he stretched out his hands towards me.

"Nate, whatever you're thinking about doing, remember—"

I couldn't even finish my warning before he lunged at me. My screams of protest and laughter mixed together as he easily lifted me and threw me over his shoulder. I could hardly breathe I was giggling so hard, and I could feel Nate's shoulders shake with laughter as he turned and started walking towards the tide.

Before I knew it, cold water surrounded me. It splashed up, hitting my face and arms as I landed in the water.

"Nate!"

"Why, Arielle, what are you doing in the water?" He leaned down, hands on his knees, peering at me as if he couldn't figure out how I'd just stumbled into the ocean. "Would you like some help?"

Laughing still, I placed my small hand in his large outstretched one. He yanked me up—hard—and I fell into him, and this time my laugh was nervous.

"You are crazy." I looked into his eyes, meaning every word.

He smiled as he leaned down and placed a gentle kiss on my forehead. "Maybe. Or maybe I'm crazy about a girl."

I grinned, leaning up and giving him a kiss. No matter how many times I kissed him, it always felt like I was soaring. Like my heart was going to explode from the way it pounded in my chest.

When I pulled back, I pushed him away playfully. "That, my friend, was a cheesy line."

He just smiled. "But effective."

I smiled back. It was true. I suddenly realized how, despite our hours of conversation and being together, there was one important question I still hadn't asked him.

"Nate?"

He was distracted, twirling my now wet hair around his fingers. "Hm?"

"What do you want to be when you grow up?"

Surprise turned to laughter as his hand dropped from my hair.

"It's a very important question, and you haven't mentioned anything about your future. Are you hiding your lifelong dream of being a beach bum?"

Now he tilted his head back as he laughed. I loved the way he gave himself to the joy he felt. He lived in the moment, and when he felt something, he expressed it. I was the opposite. I held all my emotions inside until they burst out right when I wished they wouldn't. I always knew how Nate was feeling. It was the one thing I could count on, while the rest of my future was a big, hovering question mark.

"Really? You think I would just live on the beach and surf all day?"

"Well that's pretty much what you've been doing since I got here." I smiled playfully, letting him know I was joking.

He turned, putting an arm around me and walking me back towards Sarah's. "I'll have you know that every morning, while you're still fast asleep, I'm hard at work giving surfing lessons."

I looked up at him in shock.

"I know, I know. I'm not really the teacher type, but it helps free up the rest of my day to be with you."

My heart melted.

"No, no. I'm just surprised you never told me." I looked down, feeling suddenly like I'd been so wrapped up in the attraction I felt to him that I hadn't taken the chance to learn all the little things about him. "I just want you to tell me what makes you happy."

"Well, if you remember our first stargazing expedition, that's kinda a long list." He laughed, hugging me close as we slowed our pace a little.

I think we both wanted to savor any time we had alone.

"You sure you want to know the full list? It might make you rethink being with me."

"Oh, I'm with you now?" I teased. "I'm so honored—"

"Nathan!"

I whipped around to find the owner of the shrill, high-pitched voice that had just called out and spotted two girls, both in just bikinis, making their way towards us on the beach. I glanced down at my soaking oversized T-shirt and jean shorts and felt the breeze cut right through me. They must be freezing.

The blonde one—who I assumed had shouted—was waving frantically, like if she stopped making herself known, we wouldn't see her. The brunette walking next to her looked vaguely familiar. She lagged behind, arms crossed. She didn't look excited for whatever was about to happen.

I looked back at Nate. His face was pale, and his gaze was bouncing back and forth between me and the supermodel blonde. He looked even less excited than the brunette.

"Nathan! I haven't seen you all summer!" she gushed, immediately putting her hand on his arm and batting her eyelashes at him.

Oh. Oh. It was like that between them, huh? A rush of jealousy ran through me. I knew he'd dated around. He'd told me. We'd talked about it thoroughly one night when I was feeling insecure about us. But there was a difference between hearing about it and seeing it. My chest tightened, and not in a good way.

"Hey, Lia. Yeah. I've been busy—" Nate started nervously, but she cut him off.

"You know, I've been waiting for your call. We had so much fun last time we went out." Lia pouted and ran a hand up his chest. It was honestly an impressive combination.

Nate's eyes turned huge and he took a step back. Her hand dropped from his chest as he looped an arm around me. I had to hide my giggle when I looked up at him—this tall, muscular surfer was totally using a little blonde girl as a human shield.

"I don't know if you two have met," Nate said quickly.

I glanced up at him, and he smiled down at me.

A little calmer, he continued. "Ari, this is Lia. We went to high school together. Lia, this is my Arielle."

Oh. We'd never talked about titles, so I guess it made sense that I wasn't his girlfriend, but that sentence was all I needed.

My Arielle.

I really was getting sappy.

And Lia was definitely getting pissed.

"Nice to meet you," I said, giving her a small smile.

Shocker, she just glared and then turned to Nate.

"Nathan, can we talk for a minute?"

When nobody moved, she glared even harder. "In private?"

I was ready for Nate's arm to drop and for him to follow her into the sunset, but instead, his arm tightened, and when I looked at him, I saw a question in his eyes. He was asking me if it was alright. I nodded, and only then did he drop a quick kiss to my forehead and let his arm fall from my waist, before following Lia down the beach a little ways. The brunette that had been walking with Lia came up beside me, and we both faced Nate and Lia as they began to talk—or more accurately Lia began to argue with a stoic Nate, motioning widely with her hands.

"So you're the one that finally tied the great Nathaniel Rentz down, huh?" she asked, chuckling a little bit.

"Um, I guess," I said warily. I couldn't place where I knew this girl from, but she definitely didn't seem as aggressive as her friend. "Have we met before?"

"Not officially. But you hang out a lot with Luke and the boys, and he's kind of my guy at the moment." She laughed again, and it was so fun and carefree.

My mind shot back to that first party, and Luke grinning at me as he wandered off with a pretty brunette. Then I remembered Nate and Kyle giving him crap about spending all his free time with some girl.

"Wait, you're the girl that's been hanging out with Luke?"

"That's me. I'm Courtney by the way. But everyone calls me Court." She shot me a quick smile.

"It's nice to meet you. I'm—"

"Oh, I totally know who you are, Ari. And not just because Luke is so close with Nate. Getting information from that guy is like interrogating a stone wall." She rolled her eyes, but I didn't miss the way her eyes lit up when she said his name. It was cute that this spunky girl was the one who'd broke through Luke's stoney personality. "Our graduating class wasn't small by any means, but Nate was no social pariah. A surfing champion, competent, not a total jerk, and looks like that?"

I gave her a look, and she just shrugged.

"He's hot, girl. Objectively speaking of course." She raised one hand like she was pleading the fifth.

"I mean, I'm not disagreeing." I tried to hide my smile, but I couldn't quite pull it off.

"Anyway, everyone pays attention to Nate. And when the guy that every girl tried to date in high school suddenly skips parties and is totally whipped for a girl that came literally out of nowhere, people are curious."

A wave of guilt hit me. I knew Nate and I had spent a lot of time together, but I'd really hoped he wasn't missing out on his senior-year summer for me.

Disturbing my thoughts, Lia shouted something and pointed to where Court and I were standing.

Nate glanced at us then moved his hands from his pockets, crossing his arms across his chest before clenching his jaw. I could tell he was holding in whatever rage her comment had brought on.

"It's like watching a train wreck," Court mused, tilting her head to the side as she watched.

"But you just can't bring yourself to look away," I agreed, tilting my head the same way as hers.

She turned to me and laughed. "I have a feeling we're gonna be friends."

I joined her hesitantly. I'd never met a girl so straightforward.

"Lia is my cousin, which is why I can freely admit she's crazy while also letting you know she's been in love with the idea of Nate for years. He was unattainable, and she can't stand that the girl that finally got him wasn't her."

"Oh." There wasn't much else to say. I couldn't blame her for wanting Nate—he was pretty irresistible. But her just wanting the idea of him made me realize why he'd never dated in high school. He'd always said he was waiting for me, which was cute, but I'd known there was more to it.

We were interrupted when Lia slapped Nate across the face. Like full-on, open-palm slapped him. He kept his arms crossed and barely reacted.

I couldn't say the same for me.

"Excuse me," I said as calmly as I could to Court. "I think your cousin is about to finally get that fight she's been trying to start. It's just not gonna be with Nate."

I was already stalking towards them when I heard a "Get her, girl!" from behind me.

It didn't take me long to reach them, and when I did, I didn't hesitate to push myself right between Nate and Lia.

I didn't even hear whatever nonsense she was saying because I was trying so hard not to return the slap she'd just given Nate.

"Hey, wanna keep your hands to yourself and off my boyfriend?" The words were relatively calm, but I was fuming.

She just looked me up and down, as if I wasn't even worth her time, but I was glad she did, because my fire needed a little more fuel.

"Boyfriend? Yeah right," she scoffed. "You're just some tourist who happened to get the attention of a surfer boy for a week—that doesn't make him your boyfriend. In fact, you should just take your delusional, man-stealing, psychotic—"

"Lia—" Nate started angrily, but I put a hand on his arm, letting him know I had this one.

"You know what, you're right." I gave her a small smile. "Just because you get his attention for a week doesn't make him your boyfriend. It's a good thing I've known him since I was six years old and we've been best friends just as long then, isn't it?"

She was quiet for a few seconds, and I could see the moment she decided to try again. But I wasn't done.

"You have no idea who Nate really is. If you did, you'd know that he doesn't make you guess whether or not he wants to be with you. He's so kind and beautiful it hurts sometimes. The fact that you thought getting in his face and putting your hands on him would make him get with you shows what you're really here for, and it's not for him."

Her mouth dropped open. She glanced behind me at Nate, looking for his input, but he simply looped an arm around my waist and pulled me back to his chest. Actions really did speak louder than words sometimes.

Lia glared at us one more time before stomping off without another word. She didn't even look back to see if Court was following her—which she wasn't, since she walked right up to me and Nate.

I still hadn't looked at him. I couldn't. I was more than a little embarrassed.

"Girl, you are my new favorite person." Court's smile was so big you'd never think I'd totally upset her cousin. "Putting Lia in her place without dropping down to her level? Impressive."

"Yeah, she is," Nate said softly, and I almost closed my eyes at how much his voice soothed my nerves. And my lingering anger.

"Okay, lovebirds, I'll let you recover from the drama whirlwind we all just endured." She waved her fingers and started to walk the way her cousin went. "Ari, I work at a little bookstore downtown called Seashore Books. Nate knows where it's at. Come stop by sometime—I'm there every day 'til two. We're kindred spirits, girl."

With that she winked, and a moment later it was just me and Nate.

His arm was still holding my back to his chest. I was sure he could hear how fast my heart was beating.

I'd called him my boyfriend. What if he didn't want that?

"Ari," he whispered into my hair. "Can you look at me for a second?"

I slowly turned in his arms but couldn't bring myself to look at him, so I kept my gaze focused on his chest. But Nate wasn't having it. He tilted my chin up with his knuckles until my gaze met his.

His eyes were twinkling.

"So does this mean you're finally ready to be my girlfriend? Officially?"

"You sure you want that?' I barely whispered. My heart wanted to leap out of my chest.

His eyes grew more serious as he searched mine. He saw me so clearly.

"Girlfriend doesn't even start to cover all that I feel for you, Arielle Hansen, but it'll do for now."

He smiled as he watched my reaction. I tried to hide my smile, but I couldn't. I was like a giddy schoolgirl and it was pathetic and I didn't care.

"Even though I ran right into your conversation with Lia?"

"Especially because you ran right into my conversation with Lia. It reminded me of a cute little blonde girl who always fought my battles for me when we were kids."

We both smiled at the memory of our childhood.

"It's like I'm watching you remember who you are while

becoming the woman you were always meant to be. It's pretty amazing, Ari."

I blushed at his sweetness, then before I could say anything, he got that twinkle back in his eyes.

"Oh wait. I know exactly what movie moment you're living in right now," he said excitedly as he grabbed his phone.

In a few seconds, a song started playing from his phone. He tucked it back into his pocket and pulled me back into his arms.

"Nate."

"Hm."

We started swaying to the music in something like a waltz. I held back my giggles.

"Is this the *Lion King* soundtrack?"

"I knew you'd recognize it!" He sounded so proud of himself.

"This isn't really a slow-dance song," I said, finally unleashing my giggles.

He just beamed down at me. "Yes it is. Plus, this fits the moment you're having right now."

Before I could protest, he leaned forward and quoted Mufasa in a low, somewhat inspirational voice. "Ari, remember who you are. Remember!"

I couldn't stop myself from laughing, but the laughter quickly turned to tears as what he'd said sank in. And as I thought of the scene from the movie.

"I'm having my Simba moment?"

"Yes, ma'am!"

Suddenly the music picked up, becoming fast-paced and definitely happier.

Nate looked down at me and grinned. "Ari, tempo change!"

He let me go then grabbed one of my hands in his and started spinning me, over and over. I was full-on laughing as the spins got so fast that he lost his grip on my hand. Suddenly, I was spinning alone, but I didn't stop.

I felt so free. So light.

I tilted my head back, spreading my arms and closing my eyes as I spun faster and faster.

The song turned slow and melancholy once more as it approached the end, and I slowed down and stopped spinning. When I came to a full stop, I turned to Nate. He had a soft smile on his face as he held a hand out to me. I took it and he pulled me back into a slow-dancing position, but this time he tugged our joined hands close to his chest and wrapped his arm tight around my back.

"Thank you for helping me remember," I whispered, staring into the ocean as we turned together.

He just nodded before speaking, his voice barely above a whisper. "Ari, it's always been us."

"I know."

CHAPTER NINETEEN

As our song came to an end, I realized it was by far the strangest end to a day I'd had in a long time. But I felt so content. Moving my head from where it rested on his chest, I looked up at Nate and smiled. He took his hand from my waist, pushed back my hair, and cupped my cheek.

"Photographer."

"What?" I asked, scrunching up my nose in confusion.

"You asked what I wanted to be when I grow up. I want to be a photographer." He looked away for a second, as if he was embarrassed he'd just admitted that. "I know it's so hard to make steady money being a photographer, but photos just have a way of making you feel something. I know it's stupid but—"

"It's not stupid," I said more forcefully than I'd intended.

He looked away from me again, and this time I placed my hand on his cheek, forcing him to look at me. "Nate, it's not stupid. I've seen you when you take pictures. You come alive. It's like you have this glow. And your pictures? I've only seen a few, but the ones I've seen are amazing. Seriously."

He gave me a small smile. I was normally the one so unsure, the one who needed to be told that I could. Being able to give that to Nate felt like a gift.

"It's just a dream. Maybe one day I can really make it happen."

"You will." I gave him another smile. "Believe in yourself like you always believe in me, Nate."

And then because I couldn't wait another second, I pushed up to my tiptoes and touched my lips lightly to his. That wasn't enough for Nate, because before I could pull away, he grabbed my face with both hands and pulled me back in for a long kiss.

I loved how a little bit of me was never enough for Nate. I knew I'd never be satisfied with only a little bit of him.

We were both breathless as we pulled away. The sun had fully set at this point, and the breeze carried a chill with it. I shivered, still a little damp from my involuntary dunk in the ocean earlier. Seeing my shiver, Nate stepped away and shrugged out of his hoodie then pulled it over my head.

"Oof, Nate, what—"

He popped my head through, and I started putting my arms through the sleeves.

"Sorry I didn't notice earlier you were cold." He grinned sheepishly. "Are you ready to head back?"

I nodded once, slipping my hand into his as we made our way back towards the beach house.

Once we got inside, we found Mom and Sarah were halfway through preparing dinner. From the smell of it, we were having enchiladas. I smiled at Nate. He may have said rest in peace to them, but they were still delicious.

I was already drooling.

"Hey, kiddos! Wanna help set the table, hon?" Sarah said, glancing over at us from where she was chopping onions at the counter. Her gaze dropped briefly to our joined hands, but she just smiled and continued chopping. Yeah, we hadn't said anything to the moms, but they definitely knew we were together.

"Sure thing, Ma." Nate smiled down at me, squeezing my hand tight before letting go and heading around the counter towards the cabinets. I just watched him for a second, loving how he gave Sarah a big hug as he passed by and had a smile on his face as he helped.

A second away from being a total creeper, I finally tore my gaze away from Nate and headed over to where my mom was leaning down, checking the chicken in the oven. As soon as she stood, I wrapped my arms around her waist from behind and rested my head on her shoulder.

"Hey, sweetheart. Good day?" she asked softly, and I could hear the smile in her voice.

"Yeah, really good." My mind flashed through the events of the day, landing on the one I knew would make her the happiest. "I think I made a friend today."

Mom turned around quickly, putting her hands on my shoulders as mine fell to my sides.

"Really?" There was so much hope in her eyes. I gave her a small smile. "Oh, sweetie, this is amazing!"

"Don't get too excited—we just met today and the way we met was… interesting." I ducked my head, chuckling as I relived the whole Lia encounter.

"But this is a start. A start of more than we ever thought was possible."

And with that, we made dinner. We ate together. We sang along to nineties hits as we cleaned then ended the night watching a movie together and chatting, until we all faded and made our way upstairs.

Normal was so completely underrated.

The next morning, Nate drove me to the bookstore downtown to meet up with Court. As soon as I walked through the doors, I fell in love. There were rows and rows of haphazardly shelved and stacked books, all of them second-hand, and that made me love it even more. There was something about seeing the worth in what someone else had discarded. Just because one person deemed something no longer worth their time didn't diminish the beauty left inside.

I chatted with Court as she worked at the register. Nate had stepped out "to make a quick call"—but he'd winked at me as he'd left and still hadn't reappeared thirty minutes later.

I loved that he was giving me space to make my own friend.

"I'm not saying Mr. Darcy didn't deserve Elizabeth towards the end, but I think the difference between him and Mr. Bingley is that Mr. Bingley never had to prove himself. Darcy did, like a typical man. Take that as you will." Court shrugged as she leaned against her side of the counter.

It turned out we both had a love for the classics, and we'd spent the last thirty minutes discussing everything from *War and Peace* to *Macbeth* to *Pride and Prejudice*. As many amazing qualities as Nate had, a love for literature wasn't one of them. Court was fun and spunky, and seemed to like talking with me.

"I see what you're saying, but you can also argue that Bingley didn't have as much depth as Darcy, like Jane didn't have as much depth as Elizabeth. They were content being surface level, but that never would have worked for Darcy and Elizabeth." I shrugged back at her, and we both grinned.

"I was right about you," Court said as she stood straight and went back to sorting a stack of books in front of her. "We truly are kindred spirits. And Bingley really was so unbelievably spineless, I'm surprised he even has qualities for us to discuss."

As we both burst into giggles, Nate pushed back through the door. When our eyes met, he gave me the biggest smile— like he was so happy to see me happy. I gave a content little sigh as he wrapped his arms around me and placed a light kiss on my forehead. Then he turned to Court.

"Hey, Court, Luke and Kyle texted. They're having that carnival night on the pier tonight, and they wanted to get a group together and go. Would you ladies like to join us?" he asked as he glanced back at me.

"You already know I'm ready to crush Luke's ego at the free-throw game. Count me in," Court said with an overeager grin.

"Ah, ego crushing. You really are too sweet to him, Court." Nate chuckled.

When she just gave him a nonchalant shrug, he turned his attention back to me. "What do you think, Ari? I think the moms are planning on going too, so we can all walk over together and then hang with the crew?"

I tried to tamp down my excitement. But my overenthusiastic nod betrayed how absolutely excited I was to go to the carnival. I may not have liked crowds, but I did love cotton candy.

And Nate.

I think I really, really loved Nate.

"Okay, sounds like a plan. You ready to grab some food, baby?" Nate asked me.

"Pedro's?"

"Of course. You think I'd offer you lunch and not get you tacos? What type of guy do you think I am?"

I just laughed and hugged him tight before turning back to Court, who was watching us with heart eyes.

"See you tonight, Court!" I said as Nate released me to grab my hand.

"See ya, lovebirds!" she yelled as we exited the bookshop.

When it was just the two of us, Nate turned towards me as we walked towards Pedro's, which was only a few shops down.

"You have fun?"

"Yeah," I said happily. "Luke and Kyle are great, but they're your friends. I didn't realize how nice it would be to have one of my own. Thanks for driving me."

"I'm glad." He brought our joined hands up and placed a soft kiss on mine. "You've seemed so much lighter the past few days."

"I've felt lighter." I leaned into him a bit, craving being closer to him. "Hey, Nate?"

"Yeah?"

"I'm happy."

"Yeah?" The hope in his eyes was beautiful.

"Yeah."

"So am I."

Then we ate the most delicious tacos on the planet and goofed off until night finally came.

CHAPTER TWENTY

We were upstairs, lying on the floor in his room. Don't ask me why we were on the floor. Nate had insisted it was better for digesting, and then he'd dragged me down with him. We'd been lying there for hours, just talking.

Okay, and kissing. But mostly talking.

"Ari! Nate! You guys ready?" It was Sarah calling up the stairs.

I sat up quickly, as if we'd been caught doing something other than talking and pretty innocent kissing. Well, mostly. Nate was loving this whole new forward thing we'd unlocked. But he was always respectful.

Nate just laughed at me and slowly sat up.

"Yeah, Ma, we'll be down in a sec."

"Okay! And don't forget a sweater—it's been getting chilly at night!"

Nate jumped to his feet, offering a hand to pull me up. As soon as I was on my feet, his lips were on mine. I couldn't even count how many times we'd kissed. And I still felt all the feelings overwhelming me every time.

"Alright, let's go." He smiled, and I smiled back, pulling at the edge of my hoodie. Technically it was Nate's, but I wore it more than he did at this point.

Once we'd met up with the moms downstairs, we began the walk to the pier. Sarah was excitedly chattering about the live music event happening amid the carnival night and how she was determined to force her students to study modern music in the upcoming school year.

We walked along in the darkness, with only the light glow of the pier and the shape of the Ferris wheel in the distance to guide us—then Nate was pulled away from my side to talk with Sarah.

With everything that had been happening recently, Mom and I hadn't had a chance to revisit our conversation from the farmers' market.

"Mom, I've been thinking—"

"No, honey, I will not allow you and Nate to elope. No matter how much you love him." She put an arm around me as she teased and pulled me close to her.

I laughed, enjoying her motherly touch and familiar tone.

"Mom, I-I'm not in love with him," I stuttered. I was totally in love with him, but admitting it out loud was still too scary. "And that wasn't what I was going to say."

"Darling, if you're not in love with him, then I need to reevaluate my definition of love." She laughed. "I'm teasing you, sweetheart. Now, what did you want to say?"

"Well, I'm just worried about our future. Yours and mine."

The smile faded from her face, and the worry lines that had been rapidly growing in number over the past few years showed in the faint light.

"We're almost out of money, and I don't want to be selfish, and I know I'm going to take at least a year off before I enroll anywhere, but—"

"Yes, of course, sweetheart. That isn't selfish at all. We will figure out college, I promise." She sighed, letting go of me and crossing her arms in front of herself.

As much as I hated to admit it, talking with Nate about his future had made me think about mine. How I had no plan. No real dream. I didn't know what I wanted to do, but I wanted to figure it out.

"I'm sorry to bring it up. I know you and Sarah have been having fun catching up and going out, but at some point, we need to figure out our new life." I fought the urge to fold my arms across my chest, to close myself off and run away from my problems. Instead, I put a comforting arm around my mother, just as she had with me only moments before. She smiled, leaning her head against my shoulder as we both thought of our impending future.

"Girls, hurry up! I want to ride the Ferris wheel."

Sarah's excitement was almost tangible. She and Nate had stopped, and only then did I realize how far ahead of us they'd gotten. Sarah was waving us forward, and I turned and looked at my mom. She just pulled me close, gave me a hug, and whispered in my ear before she let me go.

"Don't worry, my baby girl. We'll sit down later and figure out money, school, everything. I promise, okay?"

I tried to calm my nerves, but something felt off. Like time was running out for us to be normal. I prayed I was wrong.

CHAPTER TWENTY-ONE

When we reached the pier, the colors of the Ferris wheel splayed over everything, dancing on the old wood of the pier and the smiling faces of the people. The pier was teeming with life, hundreds of people looking at the vendors, musicians, and in line for the Ferris wheel. The carnival theme was out in full force, with booths and games scattered everywhere.

I was on the hunt for the cotton candy as soon as we stepped onto the old wood. Aunt Sarah had linked arms with my mom, and they declared they were going to ride the Ferris wheel until the music show started, and we could find them there if we needed them. Then they were off, happily chatting about some rom-com they wanted to watch.

In the crowd, with everyone pushing to get to where they wanted, Nate stepped beside me, placing a hand on the small of my back and making sure I could get through the throngs of people safely.

"I told the guys and Court to meet us at the cotton-candy machine." He spoke in a low voice close to my ear. "Figured we'd want to start there."

Even in the thick of the crowd, I couldn't help myself—I turned around, in the middle of the pier, and hugged him tightly. After we got bumped more than a few times, I finally let go and let him grab my hand instead.

"Something I said?" He grinned big.

I shoved his shoulder lightly. "You know what you did."

He shrugged. "Yep, I just like validation."

I rose onto my tiptoes, fully intending to kiss him, when we heard a shout from behind us.

"Lovebirds! Let's go!"

Court was waving us over to where she and the boys stood.

I laughed at the annoyed expression on Nate's face as we made our way over to the group.

"Way to mess with my game, Court," he mumbled when we finally made it to the cotton-candy stand.

She just shot him a look as she pulled me in for a hug. "Don't pout, Rentz. You live in the same house and can't keep your hands off each other. You'll live." She turned her attention to me. "Cute hoodie, girl."

"Thanks," I said shyly.

"Wow, she's wearing your hoodie, bro," Kyle fake whispered. "This really is big-time. Aw, he's such a big softie under that ugly mug."

I smiled as Nate started messing with Kyle, and moved closer to Court when they started play fighting. Luke ruffled my hair in greeting, giving me his usual half-smile before tossing an arm over Court's shoulders.

"Hey, Ari. Nate told us you have a slight cotton-candy obsession," he said gruffly.

Nate paused roughhousing with Kyle long enough to come up behind me, slipping his arms around my waist as I answered.

"Yep. I'm a simple girl. Cotton candy and tacos make me happy."

Nate laughed, pulling me tighter against him. "Let's get my girl some sugary happiness, shall we?"

After I convinced everyone to get cotton candy with me, we started wandering the booths. It didn't take the boys long to finish their cotton candy and start terrorizing us with their sticky fingers. I finally convinced Nate to just wash his hands in the bathrooms, my main argument being that he couldn't beat me in the free throw with sticky fingers. Thank goodness my boy was competitive.

We were near the ring toss when I felt someone glaring at me. It was like the heat was burning through my skin, the hatred was so intense.

Glancing over my shoulder, my gaze landed on Lia. She was standing with a group of guys and girls who all looked bored out of their minds.

As I made eye contact with her, one of the guys flung his arm over her shoulder. I recognized him instantly.

Johnny. The guy I'd punched.

Whoops.

He smirked at me, and any guilt I'd felt melted away. That sure was a match made by the devil.

Suddenly, strong arms wrapped around my waist and hoisted me off the ground. I squealed and laughed until Nate finally put me down, turning me around to plant a kiss on my lips. I wrapped my arms around his neck and nodded towards Lia's group, who'd now turned their whole attention to us.

"I think I made some enemies this summer." I gave him a small, sad smile.

Nate glanced back at them and scoffed. "Yeah, those enemies are real scary staring at us like that." He turned back to me, the sarcasm gone and concern touching his eyes. "Are they making you uncomfortable? I can go tell them to leave you alone."

"No, no it's fine." I shook my head quickly. That was the last thing I wanted. "They're not doing anything wrong. I just feel bad."

"Bad about what?" he asked, his voice now filled with confusion.

Nate had such cute puppy-dog eyes when he was confused. *Ari, focus.*

"Well, I punched Johnny in the face—"

"Which he deserved."

"Which he deserved. But still, kinda rude of me."

"Hm, agree to disagree."

"And I totally ruined whatever was happening between you and Lia before I got here."

He opened his mouth to protest, but I slapped a hand over his mouth so I could finish. "I know you say there was never anything going on with her other than a few dates, but obviously she didn't feel that way. As shown by how she slapped you across the face and lost her mind at the fact that we're dating. And she's glaring."

In sync, we glanced at Lia again. While Johnny had gotten distracted by another girl walking by—real classy—Lia was still laser focused on us. And definitely still glaring. I dropped my hand back to Nate's chest.

Turning back to me, Nate grabbed my face in his hands and looked intently into my eyes, but he waited a second before speaking.

"Arielle Hansen. Nothing ever happened with Lia for many reasons. But the main reason?"

I gulped.

"My heart was waiting for you."

I gave him a smile as his words sank in.

"I could never seriously date another girl until I'd tried with you. It's pretty much written in the stars, baby. Inevitable."

Any response I could have come up with was cut off when Kyle threw a ring right at Nate's head. Of course he had to retaliate, but he winked at me before turning to address his buddy.

Oh, my heart.

His cheesy lines were my favorite.

After getting beaten thoroughly by Luke and Court at the ring toss, Nate and I broke off from the group for a second to look out over the ocean together. I loved our friends, but I loved even more that Nate could tell when I needed a breather. I loved just being with him so much more than anything.

As we leaned against the edge of the pier, Nate seemed nervous.

"Hey, Ari?"

"Yeah?'

He started scratching the back of his head as he turned towards me. "Can I—can I tell you something?"

Now he was making me nervous. Hesitantly, I turned towards him.

He must have seen the fear on my face, because within seconds, I was in his arms and he was looking deep into my eyes.

"It's nothing bad, I promise! Or maybe it will be, I don't know. I just, I've felt this way for a long time, but after last night I knew for sure, and I knew I needed to tell you, and I wanted to earlier, but we got interrupted and—" He cut himself off and took a deep breath. "Ari, I—"

"Hello, princess."

No. *No.* I knew that voice.

Fear shot through me as I slowly turned, not willing to believe it. Everything moved in slow motion. *He* was here. How was he here?

I took him in for a second. Shaggy brown hair, tall broad shoulders. Bloodshot brown eyes and swaying on his feet. It was him.

I barely heard Nate speak. "Ari, do you know this guy?"

Darkness began to crowd my vision as a million thoughts ran through my mind.

Ignoring Nate, he reached forward and grabbed my arm. Hard. One yank and I was face to face with him.

"Hey!" Nate exclaimed.

"Time for you both to come home, you worthless excuse for a daughter."

I could smell the alcohol on his breath.

That acidic smell I knew all too well was what finally shocked me into action. I used my free hand to grab his shoulder before bringing my knee up to his groin as hard as I could.

He screamed in pain before doubling over, loosening his grip enough for me to yank my arm away. Reaching back and grabbing Nate's hand, I shoved past him and started running for the Ferris wheel. I needed to get to my mom. I needed to protect her.

"Ari! Ari, who was that? Ari!" Nate kept yelling, but there wasn't time. I needed to get to her. We needed to leave. Now.

How did he find us? And what was he going to do now that he had?

The Ferris wheel was one of the big attractions towards the front of the pier. People were giving me dirty looks and shouting at us as we shoved our way through. I didn't care.

We finally reached it just as Sarah and my mom came out of the exit. Thank goodness they were still there.

"Mom! Mom!" I screamed when I spotted her.

Her head snapped to me, and she immediately pushed past the people in front of her and ran towards me. There was fear on her face.

"Ari? What happened?"

"He's here," I said breathlessly. Fear was pulsing through me, like a living thing. Taking control. Driving my every action.

Understanding quickly took over her face.

"We need to go. Now."

"*What?*" Nate exclaimed. "What is happening, Ari? Jess?"

I turned towards him and opened my mouth to say something. Anything. I searched his eyes, trying to tell him everything I couldn't say.

Sarah caught up to us, grabbing Nate's arm, Mom gave her a knowing look.

"I'm sorry," I whispered before turning back to my mom.

With a small nod from her, we ran.

CHAPTER TWENTY-TWO

The stretch between the pier and Sarah's house seemed to go on for miles. When we finally reached the house, Mom muttered instructions before we broke off to frantically gather our things.

As I was rushing around my small room, gathering anything we might need, Nathan burst through the door. He and Sarah must have been close behind us. I turned, seconds from breaking down as I looked at the boy I loved so much it hurt.

"Ari, what's going on?" He was angry. He was concerned. He didn't deserve this.

"Nate." I didn't even know where to start.

"No, Ari. No more excuses, no more putting it off." He looked at the bag on my bed. "Wait, are you leaving?"

"Nate, I have to leave. That man, the one on the pier, is the reason we came here. The reason we're running."

"What do you mean? Is he dangerous? We need to call the cops—"

I had to lunge forward, grabbing his hand before he got out the door.

"No, Nate, listen to me."

He turned, his eyes as stormy as the seas.

"I've wanted to tell you for a while, but I didn't, I just—I didn't want to burden you with everything."

He let out a breath, and I knew if I didn't tell him now, I might never have the chance.

"His name is Mark Stewart." My shoulders slumped as I took a deep breath. "He's my stepfather."

"Your stepfather?" Nate said slowly.

"I lied when I said we never came back because it was too expensive. It was a lie we told ourselves."

Confusion still covered Nate's face.

"Mark is an alcoholic. That much was clear soon after he married my mom. But then he started doing little things, like taking away Mom's access to their joint bank account. Forcing her to quit her digital design job. Tracking our phones. And not just our locations—he was aware of every text, every call, every photo. Then he installed cameras and a security system only he had access to. If we ever questioned him, it would become a war zone."

I gulped as understanding started to come slowly into those beautiful blue eyes. "We lived in a tense balance of walking on eggshells and total submission until I started high school, then as soon as my freshman year started, it's like his paranoia and need to control us got even worse. We were only allowed to come and go when he said so. We were prisoners in our own house."

I took a deep breath—I hadn't ever wanted to share this next piece of my life. The piece that had scarred me more than anything. "He was always mean. To both of us. He told me I was such a princess, I was worthless, I should never have been born if I was just going to be such a burden. Things like that. He gave me a lecture on my worthlessness almost every night. But it wasn't until the week I graduated high school that he started beating us with more than his words."

Nate's eyes flashed with anger now.

I sat with a thump on the edge of my bed, my legs seconds from giving out on their own. It felt like a physical weight was crushing me, pushing down on my head, and trying to put me through the floor.

"It was only a few days, but he threatened to kill my mom if I told anybody. He'd made that threat for years. And he threatened Mom he'd kill me if she told anyone. And we believed him. But one night, I heard her scream and came downstairs to find that he'd shoved her to the ground. He was going to beat her. Again."

Nate was silent. I couldn't meet his gaze, but I felt his eyes on me.

"So I grabbed the first thing I could find. It was an urn on our mantle. It was the one thing Mark didn't know about; one of the few secrets we had from him—that it held my dad's ashes. And it knocked him out long enough for us to escape."

Nate was still silent. He was processing. I hadn't explained everything. How we'd had a bag packed and an escape plan for months. How I'd blacked out for the first time and Mom had gotten us out of there, dragging me into the car until I woke up. How terrified Mark was that if I ever left for college, I would tell someone.

I stood slowly, wanting to give him space. Waiting for him to realize how broken I was. I'd been a captive for years, broken down day after day until I was a shell of a person. Nate had brought me back to life. But that didn't change what Mark had always said about me. And given how long we were stuck in that living hell, he was right—I was weak.

I stopped, breathless. Nate hadn't moved.

Suddenly, he walked right up to me. "Why didn't you tell me?"

I wanted him to scream. I wanted him to yell at me. But instead his soft whisper tore my heart into a million pieces.

"I could have helped. Why haven't you gone to the police?"

"Nate, the police can't help us. He's in the FBI. And he's smart. Smooth. They wouldn't believe a word I said. I have no evidence."

His eyes opened wide.

"But he's not going to take the chance they would. That's why he's still chasing us. He needs to keep us quiet even more than he needs to control us. He was involved in some sketchy things. I—I only know pieces, but it's bad."

I thought of the papers I'd found. The late-night visits from scary people. All the fear and panic rushed back to me, and I couldn't breathe. I had to leave. I had to run. I pushed past Nate, zipped up my bag, and started towards the door.

"No."

I stopped, but I didn't turn. His voice had immobilized me.

He raised it with every word he spoke. "Ari, you're not going to run. We can figure this out."

I turned, sadness overtaking any fear I felt. "Nate, we can't. I have to—"

"Whatever we have to do to stop him, we can do it. I won't let him hurt you anymore." He suddenly looked like the little boy I'd left behind all those years ago. "Ari, I love you."

We stood in silence for a moment. I wanted to tell him. I wanted him to know that I loved him too. That I was so hopelessly in love with him that it hurt. That I was leaving to protect him. But I knew that if I did, he would never let me leave. His hands were curled into fists, and he was ready to fight anything that was coming. And I wasn't going to let him do it.

I dropped my bag, and in two steps I was in his arms. I kissed him with everything I had. I needed him to know how I felt, even if I couldn't say the words. I titled my head, pushing and pulling as the kiss changed. When it got sweeter, I knew that leaving him was going to hurt me more than Mark ever could.

With that thought in mind, I pulled away. Our foreheads rested against each other as we both tried to catch our breath.

Nate reached a hand forward, wrapping his fingers around the necklace he'd given me.

The broken shell.

"Nate," I whispered. "It's always been us."

He gave me a small smile. "I know."

"I can't let you get hurt. I can't. It would kill me." I gulped, my voice straining to stay even. "You have to let me go."

Before he could protest, I let go then picked up my bag and walked out the door, ignoring him calling my name over and over.

Tears slowly began to fall as I made my way downstairs.

"No!"

I'd barely made it to the kitchen when the scream reached me. Dropping my bag, I raced towards the front door.

Mom and Sarah stood, clutching each other on the front porch. And there he stood, not five feet away. With a gun raised to my mom as he staggered slightly.

"Jess, don't make this harder. Just come home, like a good wife," he slurred.

Him being drunk was of no advantage to us. It was like he was even more determined and even more aggressive when he was hammered.

Darkness started to crowd my vision again, but I couldn't black out right now. Not when my mom needed me.

Breathe in. Hold. Breathe out.

Breathe in. Hold. Breathe out.

"Arielle. The princess. The adults are talking. Come to get in the way again, have ya?"

His attention turned to me. And so did his gun. The hatred in his eyes made me sick. Mom's horrified eyes locked with mine, then she glanced at Mark before motioning for me to go back inside. I shook my head slightly, unwilling to leave her.

"Come down here, girl. It's time to go."

His voice was gruff, and I could feel his desperation from here. Maybe I could stall. Maybe it could give us time.

"Why?" I asked slowly. "Why do you want us to come back so bad? You hate us. You hurt us. Every day you hurt us."

He blinked. Then he laughed—threw back his head and laughed.

"Princess, come down the steps."

I hesitated. That split second was all it took for him to raise the gun in the air and shoot.

Bang.

Sarah screamed, and the gun was back on them.

"That was a warning. Come down the steps, or I'll let a few more bullets fly."

I glanced at my mom; I could see the fear in her eyes. I started down the steps when I heard a shout behind me.

"Ari, no!"

No, no, no. He should have stayed upstairs.

"Boy, you better stay back. Or your precious Ari will be dead before you can scream." He laughed again. "Nobody try to be a hero. Now, you want answers, princess? Get over here."

I quickly walked down the last few steps and came to a stop a few steps away from Mark. Taking a deep breath, I met those muddy brown eyes. They were filled with so much disdain. So much hatred. So much disgust.

"Why?" I whispered. Tears were starting to form, but I couldn't let him see that.

"You think you're special, little Ari? You think you and your mother mean something to me?" He waved the gun towards

Mom. "You were supposed to be submissive. Obedient. A perfect cover. But no, you had to be stubborn. You had to be a runner."

Before I could react, his arm shot out, twisting me and pulling my back against his chest, pinning me in place. I barely heard the screams as cold metal hit my temple.

"Let her go, Mark! We'll give you anything, please! Please!" Mom screamed as she dropped to her knees.

Sarah held her as she screamed, and Nate looked ready to make the world burn. I could see the wheels turning as he met my eyes. I gave him a small shake of my head.

"You both are more trouble than you're worth," he sneered, pressing the gun harder against my head as he gripped my arm tighter. "And you know too damn much. But you know what? I might just be a genius, because I know the perfect solution to all this."

We all waited in suspense as he began backing up, taking me with him.

"You want your daughter to stay safe? You keep quiet."

We'd backed up to a silver van, one I hadn't noticed before.

"Little Ari here has always been a runner. I could always keep tabs on you, Jess. But Ari? We can't have a liability now, can we?"

He put his disgusting mouth right to my ear as he spoke, and I shuddered at the feeling.

"Here's what's going to happen." He spoke loud enough that everyone could hear. "Jess, I don't need you anymore. In fact, it would be best if you're never seen again. But I know you won't make any more messes, because if you do, I'll know. And Ari will suffer for it. Because she's coming with me."

"No!" Mom screamed.

"Let her go!" It was Nate this time. "You think you can just take her? You think you can take her away and we won't come for her?"

His voice was angry, and he cleared the final steps of the porch with his fists clenched tightly at his sides. His eyes blazed, and I was stunned by the fury I saw there. Fear shot through me as the gun pressed even harder into my head.

"Come any closer and I'll get rid of my problem in one shot," Mark snarled.

That stopped Nate in his tracks. He looked at me, his gaze boring into mine as I tried to tell him to back away. I tried to show him with just a look how much I needed him to not get hurt right now.

Suddenly, the door slid open, and I was tossed inside the van before I could even react. I hit my head hard on the floor. Stars crowded my vision, and it took me a second to realize that the seats were missing. And the carpet. There was only metal flooring.

There was some commotion outside as the van started moving. My head throbbed, and opening my eyes caused flashes of pain.

Taking a deep breath, I finally got my eyes to stay open and looked right into the barrel of Mark's gun.

"You try anything, you die, girl," he snarled. "I should've killed you both when I had the chance. But you just had to bring more people into it, you and your sentimental—"

A string of curses flew out of his mouth as the van jarred sharply to the right. Then we were speeding even faster as Mark's full attention went to the road. Even with my head pounding, a thought was fighting its way to the front.

This is your chance. This might be your only chance.

I shuffled towards the door and got into a squat position before glancing towards Mark. His eyes were still on the road, curses still flying from his mouth.

I grabbed the handle of the sliding door and quickly flung it open. It wasn't even locked.

"Don't you dare—"

I barely heard the rest of the sentence as I jumped.

The ground came at me fast—I barely had time to cover my head and curl as I hit the gravel.

Gravel.

We were further from the house than I'd thought. Scrapes covered my bare legs and hands, and I felt a trickle of blood starting to run down my face; Nate's hoodie had protected my arms from most of the damage. Reaching up to my head as I slowly got to my knees, I discovered the bump that had started to grow from hitting my head on the van floor had definitely split when I made contact with the ground.

I wheezed, trying to catch my breath as pain shot through every part of my body. A quick scan said nothing was broken. At least nothing I could see—breathing was really hard.

Tires squealed as the van slid to a stop in front of me. But that wasn't the sound I was focused on. I was listening to the sirens—police sirens.

And they were close.

Mark jumped out of the van, fury in his eyes as he stalked towards me.

I tried to push up onto my feet and staggered back a few steps. He grabbed my arm and yanked me towards him.

A punch landed on my jaw before I was pulled towards him again. Another struck me in the eye.

I couldn't react. I couldn't breathe.

My vision refocused on my living nightmare.

His eyes were crazed; sweat dripped from his hairline, coating his face.

He'd snapped.

Maybe he'd always been like this. Maybe he'd never been whole.

"You really do have a death wish!" he screamed in my face.

I shook in fear. I couldn't move. Especially not when the gun was raised. Especially not when the cold steel rested between my eyebrows. Especially not when his finger tightened around the trigger.

My eyes closed in defeat.

"Sir, put the gun down!" a voice yelled from behind Mark.

My eyes shot back open. I'd forgotten about the sirens.

CHAPTER TWENTY-THREE

Mark's eyes grew wide. We'd been so caught up in him trying to kill me that we hadn't heard the two cop cars that had pulled around Mark's van. Both sets of cops were standing behind their respective doors.

Four guns pointed at Mark.

Two seconds for him to turn my body against his, using me as a shield. A shield with a gun pointed at my head.

The screaming continued—Mark hollered that this was none of their business; the police yelled at him to drop his weapon.

I looked at the officers, at their cars on the road, and all at once I realized where we were.

We were at the fork in the road—the one I'd always run to. The place where I'd decide what direction my life would take.

They always say you see your life flash before your eyes in life-or-death situations, and as I closed my eyes, I saw it all.

Mom, rocking me to sleep when I had a nightmare. Sarah, making pancakes in the morning as we danced to a song. Mom, chasing me through the house as we played. Smiling and laughing through my childhood. Dancing in the rain. Spinning in the sunshowers.

The images came faster.

I saw Nate. Holding hands with Nate. Sneaking out to watch the stars. How he'd carried me that night. Our first kiss. Laughing as we ate tacos—guac, sour cream, and salsa on the side. His teasing smile when I cried at *The Lion King*. The way he protected me. The way he loved me.

I saw his beautiful blue eyes. I heard his voice.

Ari, I don't want you to be a girl who stays. I want you to be a girl who feels like she can.

"Sir, I'll ask you one more time." Frustration laced the officer's voice. "Put. It. Down!"

My eyes opened again. For the first time in my life, I felt like I could stay. And I was willing to fight for it.

The next few seconds passed in a blur. Gathering all the strength I had left, I stepped on Mark's foot just as I reared my head back. When it made contact with his face, his grip on me loosened enough that I could pull the gun from his grasp and stumble away.

Once I found my footing, the officers wasted no time, surging forward to circle him.

Mark finally lifted his head to meet my gaze, a hand pressed to his face in pain. I quickly raised the gun at him, my hand shaking.

"Your turn to run."

His face fell as he noticed the officers closing in. He only made it one step before the closest one tackled him to the ground.

I still had the gun pointed at him as I watched the officers cuff his hands behind his back and start reading him his rights.

"Miss?" a deep voice said as a hand softly came to my shoulder. "You're safe now. It's okay. You're safe."

I exhaled.

Safe.

Exhaustion rushed through my body as the gun dropped from my hand and clattered to the ground. Then the world tilted as everything went dark.

"Hey, Ari, I know you can't respond to me right now. But I thought you'd want to know that Pedro's changed their special sauce. I know, I know, blasphemy right? It's actually not too bad, but you're the expert so we'll have to go as soon as you wake up... Please wake up, baby."

"Sweetheart, Nate's been losing his mind since you've been asleep. Sarah and I are now losing our minds at him. You know how it goes with that boy. He's even more in love with you than I was with your father back in the day. I was thinking, we could maybe go see the orchestra sometime. We haven't been in ages. Whenever you're ready to wake up, sweetheart. We'll go see that strange classical music you love so much."

"My sweet surf goddess, goodness we miss you! Your mom and I are going crazy without you. I won't even mention Nate. We have to practically drag him out of here so he can get some sleep. That boy. He loves you so much. I hope you know that. It's only been a few days, but, girl, we need you back. You chose to fight. I'm asking you to choose to stay. Love you, my girl."

"Baby, I can't wait for you to tell me all your thoughts when you wake up. I read this article the other day. I know what you're thinking. He can read? Anyhow, I read about this ocean therapy. Apparently it can really help with trauma and stress. I know you're super capable, but I also know being at the beach really

helps you when you're stressed. Just a thought.

"I-I don't know how much longer I can do this, Ari. I can't—I mean, I never even got to tell you how hard I fell for you. I fell so hard. It's actually kind of embarrassing.

"I cried through the entire Lion King *movie yesterday. I turned it on, I don't know, maybe hoping it would wake you up. As soon as it started, I cried. When our part came on, and our song played, I just held your hand and cried harder.*

"Wake up, baby, so you can tell me what a sissy I am. Please. Please."

CHAPTER TWENTY-FIVE

My head hurt.

Actually, everything hurt. My eyes struggled to open. My foggy brain took a minute to figure out what was going on.

Light came in from a window. I was lying down, in bed, with an itchy blanket covering my body. And there was something poking into my arm—and a different something stuck to my head.

It hurt to breathe.

Someone was holding my hand. Tight.

Finally, a familiar face came into focus.

"Mo—Mom?" I rasped. My voice hurt, like I hadn't used it in a while.

Her head snapped up, and she sprung to her feet, leaning over my bed to run a hand over my hair.

"Oh, Ari, you're awake!" She smiled big at me. Tears filled her eyes as she held my hand with both of hers.

"Wh-What happened?" I asked. I remembered the pier… Nate had been telling me something, then Mark had grabbed me. "Mark! Where is he?"

I sat up quickly and instantly regretted my decision. My head throbbed.

Mom sat down beside me, helping me steady myself before hitting a small red button on the side of my bed.

"Whoa, take it easy. You're safe, sweetheart. He's gone."

"Gone?"

There was no way. No way. But looking at my mother's tear-filled eyes, I allowed myself to hope.

"When you left Nate upstairs, he called the cops immediately. As soon as he heard me scream, he came running downstairs with the phone in his front pocket, and the video camera on. Not only did dispatch catch the entire conversation through the phone, but they got him on camera. Every threat, the gunshot, him holding you—with the gun against your—"

She choked up then collapsed into sobs as I reached forward, holding her close. A million thoughts were racing through my head.

This man had threatened me in front of my mother. As I'd watched my life flash before my eyes, so had my mom. She'd always tried to protect me, and I knew she felt the weight of what we'd been through.

She'd fallen for Mark's lies. She'd been the biggest victim of his abuse. She'd been promised a future, safety, love, a family. Instead, she was given a prison, fear, hatred, and an abuser.

I hugged her closer, thinking of all we'd been through. The years of feeling helpless were finally over. They were finally done.

"You and me, Mom. You and me," I said, tears starting to fall as I tried to grasp my new reality.

She finally looked up at me, holding my face softly in her hands. "Always—always, my beautiful daughter. I love you so much."

A nurse came through the door then and gasped, a hand flying over her mouth as she took in the scene. Mom glanced at her then placed a kiss on my forehead before turning.

"Hey, Janae, could you grab Dr. Haven for us? My daughter is finally awake."

The nurse just nodded quickly before running off.

I was confused, and Mom grabbed my hands tight with hers.

"Sweetheart, you were—" Her voice caught again, and she took a second to compose herself before trying again. "After everything that happened, you passed out. The doctor will probably be able to explain it more, but at first they thought you were just in shock. But then you didn't wake up. They said it was your body's natural reaction to all the stress and to the shock of two broken ribs and a concussion on top of that."

"Huh. Makes sense that jumping out of a moving car would have consequences, I guess," I grunted as I shifted in bed, trying to reposition myself. "They should really portray that better in movies."

Mom just gave me a look, but she couldn't hide her smile.

"Anyways, you've been asleep for quite a while. They'll probably have to run some tests to make sure everything is okay, but the doctor said everything looked good while you were out."

She hesitated. "Ari, you were in a coma for sixteen days."

Sixteen days?

A pair of blue eyes flashed across my vision.

Please wake up, baby.

"Nate!" I gasped. "Is Nate okay? And Sarah? They were here, weren't they? I heard them. I heard all of you."

Mom laughed as she tried to calm me down. "That boy really has been driving us nuts. He's hardly left your side. The only reason he's not here right now is because Sarah begged him to go home, take a shower, change his clothes, and eat some real food." She shook her head, grinning. "Your other friends have been by. Luke and Kyle, and Luke's girlfriend—Court."

My heart warmed at that. They didn't need to come. But they had.

And Nate didn't need to spend every moment by my bedside. But he had.

The door swung open, and a tall woman with scrubs and a dark ponytail walked into the room. She had an air of authority about her, and she glanced at the machines I was hooked up to before smiling at me.

"Welcome back, Arielle." Coming closer, she offered my mom a small smile. "You definitely gave your loved ones some stress, but I never doubted you. Now, I'm guessing you have questions. And I don't have answers to all of them, so, Mom, you okay filling in the blanks until Officer Johnson gets here?"

My mom gave a quick nod, and the doctor continued.

"Arielle, my name is Dr. Haven. I've been watching over you since you got transferred to the ICU. When you arrived at the emergency room, you were unresponsive. You had a nasty gash on your head and quite the shiner, along with two broken ribs. We did some brain testing, and everything looked good up top aside from a minor concussion."

She gave me another smile, and memories of the night I'd gotten those injuries flashed through my head.

"Given that you jumped from a moving car, you got very lucky."

"What happened to Mark?" I turned to Mom. "You said he's gone, but what does that mean?"

"He was arrested, sweetheart. That video Nate got? It was enough to launch a formal investigation. It didn't take long for people to start coming forward. And with my statement, as well as Sarah's and Nate's, they've got a pretty solid case. Turns out he never made it out of the FBI academy." She shook her head, and regret filled her eyes. "It was another lie to keep us quiet. So his trial will go much faster. And Officer Johnson is working hard with the DA to put him away for a long, long time."

Relief rushed out of me. I didn't know who this Officer Johnson was, but knowing we had people in our corner was everything. People who would fight for us.

It meant the world.

"When can I give my statement?" I asked. "Is Officer Johnson here?"

Dr. Haven exchanged a hesitant look with my mom. "He's on his way. But if you don't mind, I'd love to do a few reflex tests, take a few vitals, and see how you're feeling before we call Officer Johnson in here," Dr. Haven said slowly. "You've been through a lot, and you need to rest."

"Apparently I've been resting for sixteen days. I feel a little sore and foggy, but other than that I'm good," I said, taking a deep breath before meeting Dr. Haven's eyes. "I want my life back."

She nodded. "Let's get you home, Ms. Hansen."

After doing a few tests and giving me some medication, Dr. Haven finally let Officer Johnson in. My mom had called Sarah and Nate while I was doing my reflex testing, and they were in the waiting room.

I wanted Nate to be here, but I needed to give my statement first. I needed to be levelheaded. And even the thought of Nate being so close shot my nerves and sent my heart into a flurry.

"Alright, Ms. Hansen, I'm just going to ask some questions to touch on a few points we might need clarification on from the other statements," Officer Johnson said.

His voice sounded so familiar, but I was having a hard time placing it.

"But first, I'm just going to ask you to tell me everything from the beginning. Any details you can think of are helpful right now."

I glanced at my mom, a little bit of fear shooting through me at the idea of telling them everything.

Officer Johnson and his partner shared a look before he leaned forward, making eye contact with me. "Ms. Hansen, we'll go as fast or as slow as you need. Take your time. You're safe here, okay?"

Safe.

You're safe now. It's okay. You're safe.

"You were there?" It clicked. Officer Johnson had been there.

He gave me a small nod and a smile.

"Thank you. You saved my life."

"I'm just happy you're okay. And that you can be safe with the people you love again."

I nodded, taking a deep breath. Then I told them everything.

CHAPTER TWENTY-SIX

"Ari, Nate and Sarah will be here in a few minutes," Mom called from the room.

I finished pulling on a fresh hospital gown and ran a brush through my hair one more time. After Officer Johnson had collected all the information he needed, he'd promised us that we would never have to worry about Mark again and that he would be in contact.

Dr. Haven said I could probably head home in a few days. Until then, she wanted to keep an eye on my reflexes and brain activity, to make sure nothing was off.

It didn't feel real.

I stared at my reflection—there was so much to take in. My black eye had mostly faded, but I still had some light bruising, and my jaw was a gross yellow-purple. There was only a small butterfly bandage on my head, and the throbbing had gone down significantly. The lump was almost gone.

But what really caught my attention was my eyes.

Nate had once said that my eyes were always sad. It seemed ironic that despite the fact I was bruised and battered, that look was finally gone. My eyes were clear. I looked relieved; I looked lighter.

I looked free.

"Ari?"

The deep voice reached me through the door, shooting straight to my heart and piercing my soul.

"One sec!"

I took a deep breath to calm the butterflies, then opened the door slowly and stepped back into the room.

My eyes found him instantly. He was staring out the window, hands in the pockets of his board shorts. Almost as a reflex, I reached up to touch the shell necklace he'd given me. That day felt like years ago. So much had happened since.

Hearing the bathroom door shut, Nate whipped around. Those blue eyes found mine, and I took another deep breath.

He was beautiful. I loved him so much.

Did he still love me?

Nate took two quick steps towards me then stopped, holding his hands out in front of himself.

Neither of us moved—we just stood there, taking each other in. I wanted to run towards him, but his abrupt stop held me back.

Nate shuffled his feet, looking like he wanted nothing more than to move towards me. I didn't want to push him, but I didn't know how long I could hold back from him.

"Hi," I whispered.

"Hi." He gave me a small smile. "Are you okay?"

"I think so." I pushed my hair behind my ears. "Are you?"

"I don't know," he whispered.

He took a few more steps towards me then stopped suddenly again. "No, I need to get this out. And I know if I don't say this now, I never will. If I hold you like I've been dreaming about, we'll never have this conversation because I need you in my life too much.

"You chose to leave. You chose to leave me."

"I know." The hurt in his eyes cut through me. "I'm so sorry, Nate. I never meant to hurt you. I only ever wanted to protect you. I just love you so much, and I need you, and I couldn't—"

"Say it again," he said, cutting me off.

I looked at him, confused. "I never meant to hurt you."

He shook his head, and when he looked at me, the twinkle was there. It clicked.

"I love you, Nate. I love you so much it's hard to breathe. I think I've always loved you. It scares me, but I can't help it. You have my heart. It's always been yours, but now I finally feel like I can give it to you. Because now I can stay. Nate, I can stay."

He was beside me in three steps, throwing his arms around me and hugging me tight. I gasped as I tried to return the hug. A tiny shot of pain hit me.

"Ow, Nate, ribs!"

He stepped back quickly. "I'm so sorry—are you okay?" he asked, scanning my body.

"Yes, yes." I stepped forward, wrapping my arms around his neck. My fingers worked their way into those soft curls at the base of his neck. "I love you, Nathaniel Rentz. I'm never leaving you again."

"Good," he whispered, settling one hand on my waist and bringing the other one to softly touch my cheek. "You scared me, baby. I thought you'd left for good this time. I was scared you wouldn't choose to come back to me."

He took a deep breath, glancing down at our feet.

"I'm here, Nate."

"I know." He brought his eyes back up to mine. "I just—I need you to know. I see you, Arielle Hansen. You tried to hide from me, but you can't. Because I see you. I love you, and even before everything happened, I knew it. You are everything. You are more than I could ever deserve."

A tear slipped down my cheek. Nate used his thumb to wipe it away, before leaning his forehead against mine.

"Nate?"

"Yeah?"

"I think I want you for forever."

I felt his smile as his mouth came closer to mine. "It's a deal."

Then our lips finally met. He was gentle, since I was still a little sore. But that gentle, sweet pressure of his mouth against mine was everything. Because the way Nate saw me was more than I could ever dream of. In those deep pools of blue, I could finally see myself through his eyes. He saw the broken pieces, he saw kindness, he saw everything that I was. He saw someone worth fighting for.

He understood me. He was my home.

In his eyes, I found myself.

"Okay, my darling son. You've had your time—move over so I can hug my sweet surf goddess!"

We'd barely pulled away before Sarah came barreling through the doors.

EPILOGUE

"See ya later, Nicole!" I waved as I grabbed my bag and headed for the door.

"Bye, Ari! You back tomorrow?" the sweet high-school-aged girl behind the counter asked.

"Yep. Now that my classes have wrapped up for the summer, I have all this time to spend right here."

We shared a laugh as I pushed out the door, giving her one last wave.

Standing outside Seashore Books, I took a deep breath. I loved working part-time at the bookstore. It was a fun way to spend my time. And since my college classes were online, I was able to be flexible with my shifts. Especially now my mornings were occupied giving surf lessons.

My bag started to buzz, and I dug around until I finally found my phone. Smiling at the name flashing across the screen, I pressed "answer" as I took a left and headed down the street.

"Hey, girl! What's up?"

"Girl! You are the worst texter I've ever met," Court complained through the phone. "It's a good thing I love you enough to call."

"Uh-huh. We both know you'd call anyway."

"Whatever. Are you guys still good to go out this weekend?"

I could practically hear her bouncing as I pulled the front door to Pedro's open.

"Luke is excited to be back in Avila Beach for the summer. UCLA is fun, but we miss all you guys!"

"We miss you too! And Kyle texted and said he's gonna be here on Sunday. Apparently his mom wanted to stay an extra day in Florida after his classes finished."

We both laughed as Pedro gave me a big wave from behind the grill. Kyle had been dreading his mom coming to visit him at college for months. Her extending their stay was driving him nuts.

"Hey, I'm picking up some food at Pedro's. Can we chat later?"

"Of course! I know today's kind of a big day for you and Nate. Hope everything goes well for you lovebirds. Love ya, A!"

She made kissy noises into the phone, and I just laughed.

"Thanks, I'm hoping so too. Love you too, C. See you this weekend!"

As soon as I hung up, a big takeout bag landed in front of me on the counter.

"For the special couple." Pedro smiled as he pushed the bag towards me. "Enjoy, Miss Ari!"

"Thanks, Pedro!" I smiled as I handed him the cash, then grabbed the taco and special-sauce goodness. Of course, there were two containers each of salsa, sour cream, and guacamole on the side.

As I drove down the long road, I thought of how much life had changed in the last year. After legally divorcing Mark, Mom got everything—all the money, the house in Kansas, the car. She'd sold our Kansas place then used that money to buy a house five minutes from the Rentzes' beach house. Although, it really felt like we shared the two houses. The four of us flowed between the two so much it was like they were one.

The trial had been the hardest part. Testifying to everything with Mark sitting there, glaring into my soul, had been terrifying. But instead of looking at him, I'd focused on Nate. On my mom. On Sarah. On my future, as my past was put away for a long time. The number of illegal activities that man had been involved in was astounding, and the number of enemies he'd made in the process was impressive. It was over. And we'd moved on. With some professional counseling and a lot of good people supporting us.

I parked at the Rentzes' house and reached for my bag, pulling out a small drawstring bag I tucked into the pocket of my jean shorts before grabbing all my things and heading for the door.

When I got to the counter, I dropped my bags and stored the tacos in the fridge—we weren't planning on having dinner for a few more hours, and I wanted them to be as fresh as possible. A camera, a laptop, and some other photography gear were spread across the table. I smiled. Nate had been booking so many clients lately. He was doing weddings, couples, senior portraits—really anything he could book for now. How he managed to balance his class load at the community college and run the business more or less full-time was beyond me. But he was making connections in the industry and was shadowing a surf photographer next month.

I was so unbelievably proud of him.

Lost in my thoughts, I didn't hear the back door slide open. Suddenly, a hand looped around my waist and lips touched my neck as I jumped in surprise.

"Hey, beautiful," Nate whispered. "How was work?"

"It was good." I smiled as he trailed kisses down my neck. "I put the tacos in the fridge."

"Hm." He was distracted.

I turned in his arms, ready to say something, but his lips crashed against mine. It took my breath away every time.

He spun us around, backing me up until my shoulders hit the wall. His lips never left mine. He held my face the way I loved, both hands cradling my cheeks and his hands in my hair. I looped my arms around his neck and teased the ends of his curls with my fingers the way he loved.

"Nate," I mumbled against his lips. "We're losing daylight."

He pulled away with a groan and laid those deep blues on me. Those things were powerful.

"Nathaniel Rentz, do not give me those eyes. You're the one that wanted a sunset surf today."

"Fine." He pressed one more kiss to my lips. "You ready?"

We made our way out the sliding door, holding hands as we gathered our towels and boards and headed to the shoreline. I laughed as Nate told me all about the bridezilla he'd shot with today. I could listen to him talk for hours and never get bored. And the way he looked at me never stopped making my heart race.

After we'd set our boards down, I pulled my shirt up over my head. I pretty much lived in a swimsuit these days, with an oversized tee and jean shorts over the top.

As Nate pulled his shirt over his head, I grabbed the little bag from my jean shorts before sliding those off as well.

"Nate?"

"Yeah, babe?"

"I got you something." I dangled the little bag from my fingers.

"Ari. We said no gifts, just experiences."

"This gift is long overdue. I was a little bit of a perfectionist about it." I gave him a sheepish smile before shaking the bag around. "Come on, Nate."

He gave me a look and grabbed the bag, his eyes widening as he opened it. Then he smiled as he pulled out a piece of black string. It had a shell dangling on the end.

Glancing down at the one I hadn't taken off since the day he'd put it on me, his smile grew.

It was almost an exact match. The edges were broken differently, but it was the same color and type of shell.

"Happy one year," I whispered.

We'd argued long and hard about when the anniversary of our relationship should be, and when Sarah suggested we celebrate on the date Mom and I had come back to Avila Beach, it felt right. That was when Nate and I had truly started.

I get asked all the time if I'm okay now. If my life has gone back to normal. If everything turned out fine.

Something I realized quickly is that we'll never be fine. Maybe one day we'll be healed. Maybe one day we'll feel like it's normal. Maybe. But I don't think so.

But that's the beauty of life. Just because you carry scars with you doesn't mean you're worth any less. When you start to see your brokenness as a part of you, that's when you can truly live. And when you learn to love that brokenness, that's when you can give that piece of life inside you to someone else.

Nate never asked me to be whole. He just asked me to trust him with the pieces of myself that were broken. And I will always love him for that.

I used what I'd been through to drive my decisions. I decided to take psychology classes, aiming towards developing a type of ocean therapy to deal with trauma. To help people find the healing process I had found. And that's what I've found to be my purpose. To let the hard things change me for the better.

Nate leaned his forehead against mine. "I love you, Ari."

"I love you too."

We stood there for a second, just breathing each other in as the world turned around us.

"Ari?"

"Yeah?"

"It's always going to be us."

I smiled. "I know."

AUTHOR'S NOTE

So, I just published a book. And it was terrifying and thrilling and nerve-racking and exciting all at once.

For anyone who knows me, they know that reading is my favorite thing in the world. But writing is my ultimate therapy, and it gives the never-ending thoughts in my head a place to go. Ari's story has been in my head (and in a Google document) since I was seventeen. It is so unbelievable that her story is now out there, and I've learned so much about myself writing it. So thank you for reading and giving it a chance!

I need to thank my family, who has always supported me in everything I do and continue to bless me with helping me talk through my crazy ideas. Without their support, I don't think I would be brave enough to put my work out into the world. Huge shoutout to my parents—my mom, who is my favorite book buddy, ultimate beta reader, and the one who pushed me to publish my books, and my dad, who has always told me I could do anything I could put my mind to. Thank you for being my number-one cheerleaders and for believing in me, especially in this crazy adventure.

I want to thank my editor Laura Kincaid for being so patient with a new independent author and helping me with my (many) mistakes to bring my book to the next level. A huge thank you to Rena Violet, who designed my book cover and turned my vision into something beautiful.

And finally, thank YOU! I appreciate you reading my little book and giving it some time out of your day. I hope you enjoyed it, and hopefully you even learned something from Ari's story. If this goes well, who knows, maybe you'll see another one someday.

Ella Justice is a Tennessee girl with a passion for a good love story. She is currently earning a public health degree at Brigham Young University. Writing keeps her sane in the craziness of life. She loves hanging out with her amazing family and friends, listening to music, being in nature, and cozying up with a beautiful love story during a rainstorm. When she's not working as a tech in labor and delivery, studying for school, or reading and writing, Ella can be found watching anything and everything hockey. She is so grateful for the chance to share the stories always bouncing around in her head with the world, and wants to thank anyone who picks up her books for giving them a chance.